Transgalactic Antics

Carrie Hatchett, Space Adventurer Book 3

J.J. GREEN

ISBN: 978-1-913476-15-1

Sign up to my reader group for a free copy of *Carrie Hatchett's Christmas*, the standalone novelette in the Carrie Hatchett, Space Adventurer series, and for exclusive notice of new releases, advanced reader opportunities and other interesting stuff:

https://jjgreenauthor.com/free-books/

CONTENTS

CHAPTER ONE – CARRIE THE MAVERICK

Carrie Hatchett silently wished she had put on her thermal underwear. She had been crouching for hours in a cold, damp, trench dug by Unity troops, while the siege of the squashpump city dragged on.

'City' was a loose word to describe the squashpump municipality. It was in fact a massive mound of moist, brown organic matter on a bare, boggy plain. Try as she might, Carrie couldn't help but see it as a huge manure pile and the squashpumps as large, intelligent, civilised slugs.

"Ma bairns, ma bairns." Nearby—close enough for Carrie's translator to pick up its squeaks and transform them into Scottish-accented English in her mind—a squashpump official sat, or lay. At the beginning of the negotiations several days earlier, this squashpump, who went by the name of MacDougal, had been calm and professional, but over time it had weakened under stress and concern for its family. According to official estimates, roughly 236,000 squashpumps were being held hostage by the placktoids, a mechanical alien species intent on taking over the galaxy.

Wincing as she moved her cramped muscles, Carrie went over to the distressed squashpump and sat beside it. "I'm sure there'll be some progress soon. We'll get your children out. How many do you have?"

The squashpump reared up, lifting its upper end five or six centimetres off the ground, and sprouted multi-coloured soft tentacles. "One thousand and seventy-eight, give or take one or two. I can ne'er keep count of the wee rascals. Oh, and three hundred and twelve eggs." Its tentacles flopped. "What's t' become o' them?"

"One thousand and seventy-eight? That *is* a large family." Carrie tried to imagine what it must be like to be a parent to so many offspring. "We haven't heard from the placktoids for a while. They must be about to agree to surrender. With Unity or Transgalactic Council presence on every habitable planet across the galaxy, they don't have anywhere to go. They might be hostile, but they aren't stupid."

"Och, that's what I mean. It's taking too long. Yon evil machines are trying t' figure a way oot. They've a trick or two up their sleeves yet, I warn ye."

Carrie rubbed her chilled arms and blew into her hands. MacDougal was right. The placktoids were extremely devious. When she had been the first to uncover their illegal activities, they had fooled the Council into believing they were the victims in a dispute with the yellow liquid known as the oootoon, when in fact they had been the aggressors. But their latest plan of invading the squashpump planet had failed. Unity soldiers had driven them from every area to this final refuge. Surely they had no way out? They had no alternative but to surrender.

"How are the tunnels coming along? They must be nearly finished now," Carrie asked MacDougal.

"This evening, they say."

"I'll go and see if there have been any developments," Carrie said, hoping to find some news to calm the anxious squashpump. MacDougal collapsed limply to the ground as she left.

Not far down the trench, she found her Transgalactic Council Intercultural Community Crisis Liaison Manager, Gavin, speaking to some Unity soldiers. In their combat gear and helmets with opaque visors, Carrie found the soldiers creepy. Not because they were alien—some were human, or at least humanoid—but their uniforms took on the appearance of their surroundings, like chameleons, which made them hard to spot. She was sure one or two of them had deliberately snuck up on her to make her jump.

She waited while her huge insectoid manager finished his conversation. A cold wind circulated, and she hugged herself, looking up into the thick, grey clouds that constantly covered the sky. After a few moments the soldiers nodded at her and went away. "Any news, Gavin?"

"I am afraid we have received no further

communications from the placktoids since their most recent expression of defiance. The general consensus seems to be that positive action is required."

"What kind of positive action? Not an assault?"

"Probably, yes."

Carrie gasped. "But there are hundreds of thousands of squashpumps in there, and they're so small. How will the soldiers be able to avoid hitting them? Can't we wait until the squashpumps have finished digging the tunnels? At least then we can sneak up on them."

"We cannot afford to wait, unfortunately. We have not heard from a single hostage since this morning, and the placktoids are fully aware of the squashpumps' ability to tunnel quickly and efficiently. They know we would not use tunnelling machines because they would detect the vibrations, but that the squashpumps will dig tunnels manually to allow troops to approach the city. We are sure they can also estimate the time it would take and know the tunnels will be completed soon. A crisis point is approaching and we must be decisive."

Carrie bit her lip. On her previous assignment she had been in charge of negotiations between the squashpumps and the former tyrants of the galaxy, the dandrobians. While on Dandrobia the squashpump delegation had attacked the dandrobians, and it had taken Carrie too long to discover the real reason—that the placktoids were forcing them to by holding their families hostage on their home planet, and that the dandrobians had been in on the plot from the very beginning, for reasons no one yet understood.

"I wish I'd spoken to the squashpump delegation earlier and not allowed myself to be hoodwinked by the dandrobians, Gavin. I feel like this is partly my fault. We might have had more time to act against the placktoids and avoided this whole situation."

"Your feelings of guilt are irrational and non-beneficial. Please focus on the matter at hand."

But Gavin's news about the proposed assault was not what she wanted to take back to MacDougal. "There must be something else we can do. Can't we allow some of the placktoids' demands? Can't we just confine them to their planet, like we did with the dandrobians?"

"The placktoids' ability to create transgalactic gateways makes this impossible. We must be certain no placktoid can escape. It is confinement within the oootoon or nothing."

The mysterious, yellow oootoon, through which transgalactic gateways would not operate. Carrie well understood the placktoids' refusal to give up their only bargaining tool, the squashpump hostages. Living in air pockets within the oootoon for the foreseeable future was not a fate she would resign herself to easily, either. Her heart sank. When it came down to it, a violent end to the siege seemed inevitable. But she could not, would not, allow squashpumps to come to harm. "Gavin, we can't just let the Unity storm the compost, I mean city. We have to do something. *I* have to do something."

"I appreciate that you are concerned about squashpump safety. Such a sentiment is natural and admirable. But you must understand you are only one Transgalactic Council Officer within a large team of Council and Unity staff. You cannot and must not act as an individual in this matter. We must all obey the joint decisions made, for our own safety and that of the squashpumps."

"But I've had personal experience of dealing with the placktoids. I know them. I'm sure if I could speak to them face-to-face I could reason with them." Though Carrie had been the one to expose the mechanical aliens' devious plot, she hadn't been allowed much input into the negotiation process. This was probably because the Council was aware that taking part in long, detailed discussions was not one of her strengths, but being excluded annoyed her, and she was tired of sitting on the sidelines, distant from the action. She itched to take part and be useful.

"A face-to-face meeting would be far too dangerous," Gavin replied, "even if you were to possess the authority, which you do not. Please do not even consider such an action. It would be suicide to leave this protected position, and in the event that you did survive to approach the placktoid commander, you could seriously destabilise the negotiation process."

Carrie clenched her fists at her sides. "The negotiation process is going to be seriously destablised the moment those troops storm the manure pile. I mean city. There are squashpump babies and eggs in there. Goodness knows what the placktoids will do when the Unity starts to attack."

"It is precisely to protect the squashpumps that the Unity must attack, and soon."

Frowning at her ten-legged, bronze-carapaced manager, Carrie struggled for an answer, but she couldn't think of a suitable response. She stalked away without a word. There had to be a better way than a frontal assault. There had to be. Avoiding returning to MacDougal, she went in the other direction, towards the area where the squashpumps were constructing tunnels for the Unity soldiers.

Scanning the ground for squashpump workers, she approached a tunnel entrance. The squashpumps had created a chain to shift the earth from the tunnel, and on the far side was a great mound of excavated soil. As Carrie approached, the chain broke up, and the squashpumps began undulating and hooting. "We're there," they shouted. "We've reached the city."

A thought struck Carrie, and she made her decision quickly.

CHAPTER TWO – GOING AWOL

Sure that the squashpumps would soon report her to a Council or Unity official, Carrie sped down the tunnel. It was narrow and stuffy, barely wide enough for a human to pass through. Light from the entrance grew dim as she went deeper, and she took out the small torch she carried in her Transgalactic Council Officer toolbox: a large handbag filled with handy devices. She shone the torch ahead. The tunnel's damp walls glistened in its beam, and water dripped from the ceiling. With a trembling heart, she hoped the squashpumps had made the tunnel safe from collapse. She was getting the feeling she always got when she did something impulsive—a nagging sense of regret. At least, she hoped she would live to regret her decision.

It was warmer underground than on the surface. The air was still and moist. As she went on, the tunnel walls began to close in even more. Soon, Carrie was stooping. Her neck began to hurt. To take her mind off the dull ache and her fear that she would die alone, entombed underground on an alien planet, she tried to think what she would say to the placktoids when she arrived at the squashpump city. She shook her head and hoisted her bag higher on her shoulder.

Recalling her first encounter with the mechanical aliens, she mentally went through the different types and their roles. The placktoids,bizarrely, resembled office stationery that was common across Earth. A fact that—Carrie swallowed—meant they harboured a particular hatred for humans, who they saw apparently enslaving and maltreating their distant cousins in Earth TV transmissions shown throughout the galaxy. With a sinking heart, she realised that, as a human, she was perhaps the last Officer who should be negotiating with them face-to-face.

The main placktoid types she could remember were the ones that resembled paperclips and the massive shredders. Staple removers, staplers and ballpoint pens were some of the other kinds, but she had only seen them moving around boxes of stolen oootoon. The paperclips, on the other hand, seemed to be responsible for ship-to-surface transportation, though Carrie had also encountered smaller versions that attacked viciously. It was the shredders she had to worry about, however. They were the coordinators and commanders. No doubt there would be at least one shredder in charge of the situation ahead. A fiery anger rose up in Carrie at the memory of the shredder that had nearly killed her best friend, Dave. She took a deep breath and exhaled. She needed to stay calm if she was going to succeed in persuading the placktoids to give up the hostages and surrender peacefully.

"Carrie, Carrie, please answer immediately."

She jumped, startled by the voice coming from

her translator. It was Gavin. News must have got back to him about what she was doing.

"Transgalactic Intercultural Community Crisis Liaison Officer Hatchett, respond at once."

She winced. Her Manager knew she hated it when he called her that. She took out the translator. There was no point in talking to him. He would only tell her to go back, and she wasn't going to do that. No squashpumps were going to die if she could help it. But if she answered Gavin she would have to directly defy him.

"Officer Hatchett, answer me. Do not turn off your translator." He knew her too well. "I repeat, do not—"

Releasing the operating button on the translator, Carrie replaced it in her bag. She would need to turn it on again to speak to the placktoids and avoid hearing the piercing off-key music that was the language they used with other species, but for the time being she could escape Gavin's commands. Sweat trickled down the side of her face, due to either increasing temperatures or her racing heart. She pulled down the zip on her jumpsuit and wondered how much farther she had to go. She must be nearly underneath the city by now. Her chest tightened as she realised she had no idea where the tunnel led to. Was it right under the placktoid headquarters or on the outskirts? If she couldn't see any placktoids when she emerged, how would she find them? And if she popped up right in front of them, would they attack on sight?

Carrie stopped and, her hands shaking

slightly, opened her Transgalactic Officer toolbox. She riffled through the contents. She had never really taken a proper inventory of the devices at her disposal. There didn't seem to be any weapons in there. She sighed. She wouldn't have known how to use them anyway. Careful preparation had never been one of her strengths. Pushing her sleeves up to her elbows, she concluded that she could rely only on her skills as a Bagua Zhang master if it came to a fight.

The end of the tunnel reared up, and she had to stop abruptly to prevent herself from bumping into it. Scanning round with the torch, she confirmed she was at a dead end. Above, the ceiling looked the same as the rest of the tunnel except for some old, dead roots poking through, but Carrie was sure the squashpumps' calculations were correct and only a few centimetres of soil separated her from the city, and the invading placktoids, overhead.

Holding the torch between her teeth, she began grabbing and tearing down handfuls of moist earth. She worked quickly but quietly, unsure what technology the placktoids might have to detect sound or movement. Crumbs of soil fell onto her face and hair, and she blinked and shook them off. Then her right hand grasped at nothing but air, and light shone from above. She had reached the surface.

She squatted down and turned off the torch before putting it away. There wasn't much light from the squashpump chamber above, but there was enough to see by. All was quiet except for her heart, which thumped in her ears. Carrie pulled down more clods, creating a hole large enough for her head and shoulders. Now she could see another ceiling above, which held the source of the light. Emitting a pale blue glow, it was coated in some kind of lichen or fungus.

An object crossed her field of vision. Carrie stepped back. The object had been moving too quickly for her to identify it. Had it been a placktoid, or a springing squashpump? Though slug-like, the squashpumps could move quickly if necessary. There was another movement, and another. Squinting, Carrie tried to follow the objects, but they were moving too fast. There was nothing for it, she would have to take a chance and climb up. She decided to leap up, so that if there were placktoids in the room, at least she would have the element of surprise.

Carrie bent her knees, and launched herself upwards, throwing her top half across the floor of the space above. She slid backwards into the tunnel, the hole's edges crumbling around her, but she managed to get her knee up and onto the floor. A sharp object hit her in the face, and another hit the back of her hand. "Ow!" She closed her eyes just in time as another impacted her eyelid. "Ouch." After scrambling a short distance on hands and knees, Carrie sat up and covered her face with her hands. She was being hit on all sides by small, thin pieces of metal.

Peeking between her fingers, she confirmed her suspicion: she was being attacked by small placktoids, 'baby' paperclips the mechanical aliens had developed as part of their plan to reproduce in enough numbers to take over the galaxy. She inhaled sharply as a paperclip hit the sensitive skin between her thumb and forefinger. Peeking again, she saw her escape route through the mass of swarming, vicious miniature placktoids. In the corner of the rounded room was a hole, a dark exit.

Cringing from the attack, she crawled slowly towards the hole, unable to stand due to the placktoid onslaught. But as she neared the way out the paperclips redoubled their efforts, until it felt like she was in a swarm of stinging wasps. Gasping in pain, Carrie scrambled back to her original position. The intensity of the attack reduced enough for her to take a peek again. The baby placktoids were definitely concentrated around the hole. They were trying to prevent her from leaving. But why? Were the placktoids in the process of destroying squashpumps before the Unity forces closed in?

Carrie set her jaw. These annoying little mechanical aliens were not going to stop her from doing whatever she could to save the squashpumps. There might be lots of them, but she knew their weakness. When she had first fought them on the placktoid starship she had discovered they needed light to energise them.

Eyes squeezed shut, she jumped up and dug her fingers into the fungus growing on the ceiling. It was spongy and soft and yielded easily. Before long, she had pulled more than half of it away from the roof and put it face down on the floor so that only its dark, non-luminescent, earthy roots were showing. She was sure she felt fewer stings. She risked another look. The chamber was quite dim now. The placktoids seemed to be struggling to fly. With one eye on the exit, she grabbed at the remaining pieces of fungus, plunging the chamber into darkness.

She shuffled forwards, holding her hands out in front of her, until she found the wall. Feeling downwards, she soon located the hole. As soon as she was out, she scanned the area for signs of placktoids. The mound's interior was dingy and warren-like. There was no sign of any squashpumps or their eggs. All she could see clearly was a single light in the distance. A green light. It was only a faint trace of glowing mist, but Carrie's heart sank at the sight of it. The placktoids had escaped. They had disappeared through a transgalactic gateway.

CHAPTER THREE – CARRIE'S COMEUPPANCE

Never before had Carrie seen Gavin's razor-sharp inner mandibles at such close quarters. They filled her vision, glistening with mucus, and she struggled to concentrate on what he was saying. She caught the words irresponsible, reckless, impulsive and idiotic. She thought the last one was a little harsh. Of all the Transgalactic Council staff, she had the most experience of dealing with the deceptions of the placktoids. That was why they had asked her along. Only they had never given her a chance to use her knowledge. Maybe if she'd arrived in the squashpump mound a little sooner—

"Transgalactic Intercultural Community Crisis Liaison Officer Hatchett, did you hear what I said?"

Shuffling a little to the side so that she could look at Gavin's hundred or so eyes, which were slightly less unnerving than his mouth, Carrie replied, "Yes, every word."

"Good, please remain where you are. Your guard is approaching."

"Wh-what? My guard?" Carrie's mouth went dry and her knees weakened.

Gavin chittered. "As I have already informed you, you are under arrest until your return to

Earth. Transgalactic gateway use is prohibited while the Council tries to determine the route the placktoids followed. When we know their destination we can begin to use gateways once more—"

"Wait, wait. What was that you said about me being under arrest?"

Her manager did not answer. He reared up until he was standing on only his hind pair of legs while the other nine pairs beat the air. Carrie could smell roses, sweet and musky. Gavin was exuding pheromones, the language of his species. He seemed to have temporarily lost the power to communicate in English. Pair by pair, his legs dropped to the ground, and a quiver ran up the insectoid alien from the tip of his tail to the ends of his antennae. After another pause, he spoke. "I apologise for my outburst, but your attitude is, at times, extremely trying, Officer Hatchett.

"I repeat, your unilateral action in entering the squashpump metropolis in an attempt to negotiate with the placktoids on an individual basis indicates that you are a danger to not only yourself but also to innocent civilians and Council and Unity staff. You are under arrest. Please wait here. The Council currently has more important matters to address."

"But—"

He left without listening to her protest.

"But I was only trying to help," Carrie exclaimed, to no one. Arrested? Her muscles grew rigid. Arrested? After her act of bravery?

Outrage and anger surged through her for a moment, but then events of the long day caught up to her, and she slumped down in the trench and wiped dirt from her face, grimacing at the stinging of hundreds of tiny cuts the baby paperclips had inflicted. A sullen resentment formed in her stomach. *She* had been the one who'd seen the signature remains of the green mist that had informed the Council how the placktoids had left the planet. *She* had been the one who had been prepared to risk her life to save the squashpumps. *They* had been going to attack without caring what the placktoids might do in retaliation.

"Stand up," said a voice at her side.

Startled, Carrie looked up to see a Unity soldier framed against the sky, though his helmet and uniform were quickly turning deep grey to match the clouds overhead. He seemed to have appeared out of nowhere. "Geez, you guys. How do you do that?"

In answer, the soldier bent and roughly grabbed her arm, pulling her to her feet.

"Ow, all right, all right. I'm standing up."

Tugging her arms to her front, the soldier fixed restraints around her wrists before bending and locking similar devices around her ankles. He stood to one side, legs akimbo, while his uniform slowly blended to the colour of the trench wall behind him.

Carrie sank to the ground once again. More Unity soldiers passed, and Transgalactic Council Managers and other Council staff. Squashpumps also slid by. No one spoke a word to Carrie. It was as if she didn't exist. Resentment gave way to self-pity. She fought down the rising lump in her throat. She was determined not to cry. She had been right to do what she did. They just didn't understand. No one cared about the squashpumps more than her. The only person she had endangered by going alone to the squashpump pile was herself.

A squashpump glided to a stop. "They told me I'd find ye here."

Carrie wondered which one it was. They looked so similar.

"If I'd've known what ye were going t' do I'd ne'er have told ye aboot ma bairns."

MacDougal. Carrie closed her eyes for a moment. Her impulse was to apologise, but that would mean admitting what she had done was wrong. "I was going to talk to the placktoids and save your children. The Unity were preparing to storm the mound. Who knows what would have happened then?"

"Tsk. What ye did was more risky, and stupid. No doot aboot it. What did ye think was going t' happen? Yon placktoids would listen to ye? Ye think ye're that important do ye?"

A flush crept over Carrie's face. She swallowed. "No, I don't think I'm that important. I was just trying...I wanted to help."

"Sometimes the best help ye can offer is doing nothing. Doing what ye're told."

She could find no answer to this, and

MacDougal began to leave. "Wait." The squashpump stopped. "What about your children and eggs? Are they safe?"

"Yon mechanicals destroyed our eggs days ago, but the adults and bairns managed t' escape into the walls."

"Thank goodness. That's something at least, isn't it?"

"Yes, no thanks t' ye." MacDougal glided away.

***

Carrie's dirty face was streaked with tears when Gavin finally returned. In the hours while she waited, she wondered what they were going to do with her. Would they charge her with something? Put her on trial? Or just give her the sack? She also tried several times to talk to the guard, hoping for a friendly voice, but he never answered and only stood immobile and nearly invisible to those who didn't know he was there. She wondered at his stamina, for she was chilled through and her muscles ached no matter in what position she stood or sat. But all her fatigue melted away while she listened to what Gavin had to say as the guard released her from her restraints, and she stretched and rubbed her wrists and ankles.

"The Council have been unable to trace the transgalactic route the placktoids took, and so far there have been no sightings on any inhabited planet in the entire galaxy. It is most puzzling. There were large numbers within the metropolis. Too many to hide easily."

"They've disappeared entirely?"

"To all intents and purposes, yes. Locating the placktoids is now the primary focus of the Council's efforts. They represent a grave danger to all sentient beings. Council and Unity resources are being withdrawn from non-life-threatening disputes, and new staff are being recruited to address the crisis, which in your case is extremely fortunate."

Carrie stopped stretching. "Really? Why?"

The insectoid alien seemed to consider his words for a moment. "Perhaps against my better judgement, I argued strongly that you should remain in service."

"Oh...thanks."

"Technically, you did not disobey a directive because no order was given not to approach the squashpump city as an individual. It was assumed no member of staff would do something so foolish and ignorant."

Anger flared in Carrie. They still didn't understand.

"I pointed out that your experiences with the placktoids could prove useful in the future, and that we needed every operative we had if we were protect galactic civilisations from their threat. I persuaded the Board that with remedial training your performance might improve to acceptable standards."

Carrie frowned. Remedial training? They were acting like she didn't know what she was doing.

"This training is for poorly qualified

applicants, and it is the final opportunity for badly performing Officers to remain in employment with the Council. In truth I believe the only reason the Board agreed to it is because they currently have far weightier and pressing matters on hand. However, it is important that you understand the gravity of your error," Gavin went on, but Carrie wasn't listening.

Remedial training? She shook her head.

CHAPTER FOUR – BEGGING A FAVOUR

"Wow, what happened to you?" asked Dave as Carrie arrived by transgalactic gateway through the cupboard under her kitchen sink.

Carrie slung her Council Officer's toolbox onto a table and peered at her reflection in the stainless steel panel at the back of her cooker. The hazy image was dishevelled, dirt-smudged and inflamed with pink marks from the baby placktoid attack.

"You won't believe it." Carrie bent down to pat her dog, Rogue, who was quivering with effort as he resisted the urge to jump up and lick her face.

"Sit down," said Dave. "I'll make some tea."

With a sigh, Carrie slumped down at the table. While waiting for her tea, she related the events of the siege, the words pouring out in a torrent of outrage and incredulity. After a while she calmed down a little. She took a sip of her drink and said, "And what do you think they did when they found out I'd gone there all by myself to try a different approach? To try something other than going in there all gung-ho and risking the lives of innocent squashpumps?" Her mug thumped to the table and tea sloshed over the mug's lip and ran down the sides. "They ARRESTED me."

Dave had been riffling through Carrie's toolbox, pulling out devices and peering at them before placing them on the table. "Uh-huh." He took out another object. It was a large, thick tablet in a plastic wrapper. He held it up. "Do you know what this is?"

Carrie frowned. "No, I don't. It looks like a dishwasher tablet."

"Carrie," Dave said, "it's a Transgalactic Council Officer device. I don't *think* washing dishes is in your remit."

"Did you hear what I said? They put me under arrest. For doing my job." Her voice and eyebrows rose in indignation.

Carefully putting down the tablet, her friend paused a moment, his expression uncomfortable. "But...you weren't really doing your job, were you?"

"What? Of course I was. I'm a *Liaison* Officer. I was trying to *liaise* with the placktoids. Resolve the dispute peacefully."

Dave dug into the bag for another object, avoiding eye contact. "Well, yes, but isn't your job supposed to be doing what the Transgalactic Council tell you to do? I mean, first of all. If they'd wanted someone to go in there alone, they would have sent someone, wouldn't they?"

Carrie couldn't believe her ears. Even Dave, her best friend, didn't understand. "Just because it wasn't their idea, it doesn't mean it was the wrong thing to do." She added another spoonful of sugar to her tea and vigorously stirred it in, rattling the teaspoon against the sides of the mug.

"What I mean is..." Dave sighed and rubbed his forehead. "...it might have been better to ask Gavin first."

"That wouldn't have been very clever of me, would it? If I'd asked him he would have told me not to do it. They'd already made their minds up. *Someone* had to do something. Just because I was that someone, they decide to punish me for it."

Her friend opened his mouth to speak but closed it again. He appeared to change his mind about what to say. "So, what happens now?"

"Urgh." Carrie shook her head. "Now I have to go on remedial training. It's for new recruits and Officers who are on their final warnings. And if I don't pass, that's it. Goodbye job. Goodbye journeying between the stars, meeting aliens and having adventures. If I'm not—" she mimed quote marks with her fingers "—*trained*, I'm stuck here on Earth working in a call centre for a living. I mean, it's okay, but I want to do something more with my life." She took a sip of tea. "Anyway, the good thing is, you're coming with me."

"What?" Dave pushed his chair away from the table. "No no no." He waggled a finger at her. "Uh-uh. That's not happening. Not again. Not after last time. Flying around on ancient mythological beasts? Being chased by giant gods of Ancient Greece? No way, Carrie, no way. I ate their food and drank their drink. I could be immortal." He pointed at her. "You could be immortal."

"You say that like it's a bad thing," Carrie exclaimed. "Look, calm down, all right? It's perfectly safe. It's Gavin's idea, not mine. He said it was the only way he could persuade the Council to let me stay on. He said something about how you were clearly a calming influence on me and I could learn from your sensible, level-headed attitude." She rolled her eyes. "The thing is, now of course there's a massive crisis. They don't have any idea where the placktoids have gone or what they're doing. They want to increase the Council and Unity presence across the galaxy, so they're having a huge recruitment drive and sending all the less-qualified candidates on basic training. That's where we'll be going."

"No, Carrie, no." Dave shook his head and folded his arms. "That's where you'll be going. Not me."

"Oh come on, Dave, it's just training on board a Council starship. You won't have to *do* anything. After a week you'll be home again. You know they'll deliver us back here only a minute or two after we leave. Think of it like a holiday without having to take any time off work."

"Huh, some holiday. The answer's no. I'm sorry, I know you love it, but I'm not cut out for doing the kinds of things you do. I'm the stay-at-home type." He got up and took his and Carrie's mugs to the sink, where he washed them. Carrie frowned at his back. After placing the mugs upside down on the draining board, he returned to his chair and lifted his jacket from the back of it. "A nice, steady, easy job at the call centre. Friday nights at the pictures, Saturday nights down the pub. Two weeks in Spain every year. That's the kind of person I am, Carrie, and I'm not going to change." He put on his jacket and began to zip it up.

"Put it back."

Dave's hand stopped midway. "What? Put what back?"

"Whatever it is you've got. You took something from my bag and put it in your jacket pocket before you went to wash the mugs."

"No I didn't." But he looked uncomfortable, and a flush began to creep across his face.

Carrie folded her arms and gazed at her friend.

"Oh, all right," he said, deflating a little. He took Carrie's magnetic field neutraliser out of his pocket and put it on the table. "I just wanted to have a closer look. I would have given it back."

Picking up the neutraliser, Carrie twirled it thoughtfully before placing it carefully in front of her friend. "It isn't just your *condition* that makes you take things, is it? You've always been fascinated by my Liaison Officer's tools, haven't you?"

"Who wouldn't be? They're alien technology.

They can do things Earth scientists haven't even dreamed of. They're fascinating."

"Sit down a sec."

He shook his head and zipped his jacket to the top. "I have to go. It's late and we've got work in the morning."

"Just a minute, okay? I won't keep you."

Sighing, Dave sat down. "I hope this isn't about going on training with you. I've told you, there's no way."

Carrie held up the neutraliser and looked into her friend's eyes. "What if I were to tell you that you'd get to know what all of these things do, and how to use them? And not only that, Gavin told me our supplies were being updated with *new* devices. The very latest technology they have. They're pushing out all the stops in an effort to protect everyone from the placktoids."

Dave didn't reply. He looked from the objects to Carrie and back again.

"There wouldn't be any danger at all. You'd only have to do the training exercises with me. You wouldn't even have to pass them, just be there with me. That's all Gavin said. Just come along."

Still Dave didn't speak. He picked up the thick tablet his friend hadn't been able to identify earlier.

Carrie took it from him and put it down. She held his hands and looked him square in the face. "Please?"

He slumped like a puppet with its strings cut. "I'm going to regret this, I know I am."

Carrie grinned.

CHAPTER FIVE – ALL ABOARD

It wasn't until Carrie was standing among the candidates training to be Transgalactic Intercultural Community Crisis Liaison Officers that it occurred to her that she and Dave would be the only humans. The most noticeable individual in the group was a huge, dark green blob towards the back of the room. To Carrie's left was a small hairy creature about as high as her knee, with no face, and on her right, sitting atop a cylinder as high as her waist, was a squashpump. There was also a many-legged insect that seemed to be distantly related to her Manager, Gavin's, species and a light that flashed intermittently without any energy source as far as she could see. But perhaps the strangest Liaison Officer candidate of the bunch was a box; just a cube of deep red, shiny material. How it got about, she had no idea.

Dave was standing two candidates away, looking as though he was already regretting his decision to join her in the week-long training session. He was looking around the creamy ceramic room they were standing in aboard the Transgalactic Council starship. Carrie suspected he was trying to avoid looking at the training manager who was currently addressing them, explaining the living arrangements and their general schedule for the week. Though the manager looked like Gavin, it was a female. Carrie knew this because it had a hole in its abdomen, an anatomical fact she had learned through a painful faux pas in her previous assignment. She yawned. The manager had been droning on for at least fifteen minutes.

"Any questions?" she asked, apparently coming to the end of her introductory speech.

"Yes," said the squashpump trainee, "where will we be sleeping? And this atmosphere's too dry for ma skin. 'Tis makin' me uncomfortable."

"Do not worry," replied the manager. "All your cabins, uniforms and equipment have been designed or modified to suit your species' requirements. For example, you will find a uniform in your climatically controlled cabin that will keep your skin moist. We are quite used to meeting the ranging needs of our staff. Anything else?"

"How will we do the exercises? Don't ask that, it's obvious. Well, it isn't obvious to us. Speak for yourself. We want to know. Ask again. Yes, ask her again. No, you ask. I asked once already."

Carrie couldn't see who was speaking, but her heart leaped. The voices must have been coming from the box, or rather, not the box, but what was inside it. She had met the yellow liquid known as oootoon on her first assignment. A collection of individuals melded into one amorphous mass, it constantly argued with itself. It was wonderful to have the chance to meet it again, but she wasn't sure how it could work as an officer for the Transgalactic Council.

"Each candidate has something to offer to the role of Transgalactic Intercultural Community Crisis Liaison Officer," replied the manager. "Where an individual is prevented from completing a training exercise by its anatomy it will not be required to take part."

"Well, that isn't fair," exclaimed the hairy creature at Carrie's side in a surprisingly deep baritone, though she couldn't figure out how it was speaking. "We should all do the same training. How are you going to tell who the best candidates are?"

"Let us be clear. The galaxy is home to hundreds of sentient, civilised species. Each possesses skills that are useful to the Council. Excluding a species because it cannot complete a certain task means the Council is deprived of other benefits it offers. Consequently, during your training we may not be assessing which of you perform the best in any given exercise, but who are best suited to the role of Liaison Officer. Your tasks are a means for us to observe your skills."

Great, thought Carrie. *Why do they have to make it complicated? Why can't they just tell us what they're looking for? Then I can show them I can do it.*

"More questions?" asked the manager. After a pause it continued, "No? Then you may go to your quarters and settle in. The doors on this starship are activated by pheromones or genetic signatures. The entrances to your allotted cabins have been programmed to open to only your touch, and your partner's if you are sharing. Training rooms and other common rooms are opened by pheromones. Your translators will produce them if you hold them up to the doors. A map and key to the door symbols and your individual itineraries are on your briefing devices."

The group of trainees began to break up, the box of oootoon rolling on hidden wheels towards the door. Dave was already rummaging in his bag, looking like a child on Christmas morning. Carrie went over to him. "Let's go to our room. You can have a proper look at everything in there."

"*Our* room?" Her friend stopped what he was doing.

"Yes, they've put us together. Didn't you know?"

"Oh."

"What's wrong? Do you snore or something?"

"Transgalactic Intercultural Community Crisis Liaison Officer Hatchett, how pleasant to see you again." The training manager had come over as the group dispersed.

"Oh, yes, you too," replied Carrie, confused. Had she met the insectoid alien before? The only two she knew were Gavin and... She sniffed. She could smell a faint spicy vanilla scent. It couldn't be...? "Errruorerrrrrh?"

"My English name is Errruorerrrrrhch, yes."

"Wow, I mean, good to see you." Carrie

struggled to reconcile this apparently friendly alien with the Transgalactic Council Manager who had given her such a hard time on her previous assignment. Errruorerrrrrhch's beef had actually been with her former lover, Carrie's boss, Gavin, though that hadn't prevented her from taking it out on Carrie. "But, I thought you couldn't speak English."

"I apologise. I may have allowed personal feelings to intrude upon my professionalism in the past. I am able to speak English, but I am afraid I chose not to at the time. But let us put all that behind us now. I hope to establish a good working relationship with you henceforth."

"Sure, of course."

"Allow me to show you and your companion to your quarters."

"Thanks."

Carrie and Dave followed Errruorerrrrrhch through the maze of tunnels to a recessed door that looked the same as all the others, only with a unique set of symbols outlining it. Carrie tried to remember the route but wasn't sure she could. On the way, the manager had chatted with the two humans, praising Carrie for her ingenuity in uncovering the connection between the dandrobians and the placktoids. Carrie could hardly believe this amiable insectoid alien and her former manager were the same individual.

As Errruorerrrrrhch left, saying she would see them at breakfast, Dave placed his hand on the door and after a moment it opened. Inside was a room similar to a cabin on a cruise ship, containing twin bunks, low lockers, and a small shower room. The bags they had brought with them from Earth and two bright orange Transgalactic Council Officer uniforms had been placed on the beds. Best of all, in Carrie's opinion, there was a window. Beyond it, a starscape shimmered. Her breath caught in her throat. "It's wonderful. Perfect."

Dave sat on the lower bunk. "Can we put a curtain over that?" he asked, gesturing towards the window.

"Why? It's a beautiful view."

"I don't think so." He went to the window and looked out. "Space is so cold, and dark, and..." he grimaced, "...endless."

There was a buzzing sound at the door. Carrie placed her hand on the surface, and as the door opened, she took a step back.

"Bloody hell," said Dave, the colour draining from his face.

"Carrie, I am pleased to inform you I will be present for the duration of this training exercise."

It was Gavin, but it was more than Gavin. Crawling over every inch of his surface were hundreds, perhaps thousands, of smaller Gavins. As he spoke, one crawled out of his mouth. Carrie gave a small scream.

"You appear to be disturbed. Please be assured, there is no cause for alarm. I would like to introduce you to the bounty of my union with your former Manager, Errruorerrrrrhch."

"These are y—your and Errruorerrrrrh's k—kids?" stuttered Carrie.

"That is correct. We have not yet named them all, otherwise I would introduce you. Stop that, you little scamp." Gavin appeared to address the comment to a tiny insectoid alien swinging from one of his antennae. "In our species the father cares for the offspring until the first moult. I thought it would be pleasant to be here during the training programme while I am on paternity leave, and fortunately the Transgalactic Council agreed to my request."

"Fortunately," muttered Dave, who was backed against the rear of the room.

CHAPTER SIX – DINNER DIVERSIONS

"You can't put your stuff there. My stuff's there," said Dave.

Carrie eyed the surface of the locker nearest the bunks, where Dave had arranged the entire contents of his Transgalactic Officer bag into neat rows and columns, all the items spaced equal distances apart.

"Well, where can I put my bag, then?"

"Over there," said Dave, pointing to another locker on the far side of the cabin. "That's yours."

"But I wanted to use this one, next to the bed. Then I can reach my things without having to get up."

Dave sighed. "Well it's too late now. I put my stuff away while you were in the shower. I've organised everything."

"I can see that." Carrie threw her officer's bag across the room onto the top of the locker, where it landed with a crash.

Dave winced. "You ought to be more careful. You'll break something."

"Oh, I don't think there's anything fragile in there. With all the technology the Council has, everything's bound to be pretty tough."

Her friend didn't answer. He was examining one of the thick tablets he had found interesting before, when the two had been talking in Carrie's kitchen. "I'm looking forward to finding out what this is."

"It looks like a—"

"It isn't a dishwasher tablet."

"But it does look just like one, though, doesn't it? It's even got a plastic wrapper. Why don't you open it and see what's inside?"

Dave put the tablet with the rest of the items on top of the locker, positioning it carefully. "We might not be supposed to open it yet. It might be for a training exercise."

"Oh, I'm sure it's okay." Carrie reached for the tablet, but Dave pushed her hand away.

"Don't take mine. If you're going to open one, open your own."

"You're such a fusspot. They're all the same, you know." Carrie unfastened her bag and began pulling out devices, scattering them on the locker top. Two or three dropped to the floor. "Here it is." She took out the tablet and pulled at the wrapper. When it wouldn't come off, she ripped the covering with her teeth and spat out pieces of plastic. Dave watched where they landed.

"Hmph, look." Carrie held out the package contents, a grey cake of a powdery material. "It definitely looks like a dishwasher tablet. Oh."

"What?"

"It's going all crumbly." The surface of the tablet had begun to disintegrate. Carrie rubbed it, and more of the powdery material broke away. "Oh well, never mind." She tossed it onto the locker, where it broke into pieces. She put her hands on her hips. "Are you ready for dinner?"

Dave stood and stretched. "Yes, I've looked up where we need to go." He picked up a transparent piece of plastic that displayed a map. Carrie knew this gadget: it was the briefing device that held the information she needed for her assignments. She hadn't known it contained maps too.

"Great. Let's go, then," she said, sliding her translator into her pocket. She planned on getting reacquainted with the oootoon over the evening meal.

"Don't you think you should bring yours?" Dave held up the transparent briefing device.

"No, I'll be fine. I'll just follow you around." Carrie grinned.

***

Dinner for the two humans looked like spaghetti bolognese, but it tasted like seaweed, and brick dust, and a graduation party hangover. It was as though the Transgalactic Council chefs had seen spaghetti bolognese but hadn't the remotest clue what went into it, and even if they had, they hadn't the slightest chance of getting the ingredients. As a vegetarian, it was important to Carrie that the meal contained no meat, and judging by the taste and the horrified reaction of Errruorerrrrhch when she'd told her about her dietary requirements—as if she was some kind of monster for even suggesting the Council would provide dishes made from animals—she was confident that it didn't.

From the look on Dave's face as he chewed, she guessed he was adding the meal to the list of reasons why he didn't want to be there. Keen to avoid his reproachful glare, Carrie turned her attention to the oootoon sitting, or rather, occupying the space next to her. The box lid was open, and the oootoon was visible within, filling the box to the brim. Sitting as she was at a dinner table, Carrie couldn't help but be reminded again of the alien's resemblance to custard, though she hadn't touched a drop of the stuff after mistakenly eating some oootoon in her first assignment. Drips of a white liquid were falling from a pipe on the ceiling. Surely it couldn't be milk?

"It's so wonderful to see you again," she said.

"Hello, who are you? It's that alien, from the time with the placktoids, remember? No, I don't. Me neither. I wasn't involved in any of that. The one in the placktoid starship. You must know. Oh, yes, we went up, didn't we?"

"Yes, that was me," interrupted Carrie. "And Dave was there, too." She glanced at her friend, who was munching stoically. "You protected us when the starship crashed. And my boss, Gavin, and my colleague, Belinda. I wanted to thank you. With everything that was going on, I forgot to. You saved our lives."

"Did we really do that? You're welcome. I think so. No problem. Anyone would have done it."

The clatter of cutlery hitting the floor distracted Carrie. Dave had dropped his knife and fork and was staring, white-faced, at the doorway. Gavin had arrived and was heading in their direction.

"I—I'm full," said Dave. "I'll see you back at the room," he spluttered before darting to the wall and, as Gavin approached, edging along it towards the exit. As soon as Gavin was safely in front of him, he bolting through the door. The insectoid alien manager had brought his babies along. They leaped and ran all over him, occasionally falling off then climbing up again. Carrie wondered how he moved under all the additional weight, but his offspring didn't seem to bother him at all.

"Hello, Carrie," said Gavin, "I thought I would find you here. I hope the human food is to your liking?"

"Well, it's…I'm sure the chefs tried very hard —"

"Good, good. Oooh, that tickles."

Carrie assumed the second remark was addressed to one of his children.

"I am not hungry myself. I will not eat again until these little rascals have moulted. I came here merely to reassure your friend, Dave, about the first test, but he seemed to be in rather a hurry to leave. His character is rather different from yours, being more circumspect and cautious. It would be natural for him to feel rather wary of invasive procedures, but the examination is entirely harmless. Would you tell him for me?" The alien's head swivelled round as Errruorerrrrrhch entered the canteen. "Oh my goodness, I must leave. Do pass on my message, please. I would not want Dave to be unduly concerned."

"Yes, I—" said Carrie, but Gavin was already scuttling away towards the opposite exit, taking his hundreds of offspring with him. As Carrie wondered why he was avoiding the mother of his children, Errruorerrrrrhch addressed the Transgalactic Council Officer trainees.

"I apologise for interrupting your meal. I have a small announcement. We have made a minor change to the itinerary. Due to the placktoid threat and the accompanying necessity of expediting your training, we will be conducting the first test, a deep brain scan, tonight while you sleep. This test measures the type and extent of nerve connections within your brains or other neural systems of your species, and the results indicate your general ability in the position of Liaison Officer. This is a starting point for us to determine how you might best work within the role, and which features of training will be of special benefit to you."

Deep brain scan? Carrie frowned as she picked up her fork and twirled the awful spaghetti-like substance around it. Scanning brains seemed an odd way to assess someone's skills. What would the test tell them about her? She had no idea, but she didn't like the sound of it. She had always thought she was more sporty than brainy. Why couldn't they just let her show them what she could do?

***

For the rest of the meal and some time after, Carrie chatted with the ooootoon—with some difficulty—and got to know the other trainees. The large green blob was especially friendly, but the flashing light was quite standoffish, she thought.

When she got back to the cabin, Dave was already asleep. She decided not to wake him up to tell him about the brain scan. There was no point in worrying him unnecessarily. As she got ready for bed, she noticed the room looked a lot tidier than she had left it. The floor was clear, and all her Liaison Officer devices had been placed neatly away in her bag..

CHAPTER SEVEN – BRING OUT THE BIG GUNS

When Carrie woke, she could hear Dave in the shower. She dozed back off to sleep while waiting for him to finish. The sound of the door opening jolted her awake again. She sat up, stretched and yawned. "Did you get a good sleep?"

"Not bad." Dave was filling his bag with his Liaison Officer devices. "You'd better hurry up. Breakfast will be over soon."

"Oh no." Carrie swung her legs over the edge of the bunk and jumped down. "I'll have to miss it then. I won't have time for a shower otherwise."

"You can't have a shower. I've just cleaned it. And you shouldn't miss breakfast. It's the most important meal of the day."

"What? Why did you clean it? It's a shower. It's already clean."

Dave narrowed his eyes at her. "No it isn't. Anyway, you had a shower last night. I thought you wouldn't have one this morning too."

"Of course I'm going to have one this morning. What do you think I am? Dirty or something?"

Dave opened his mouth to speak but changed

his mind. He took a comb from his bag and began to comb his hair in front of the mirror on the wall above her locker. He looked fantastic in his fluorescent orange uniform, as Carrie had known he would. She sighed as she remembered how hers made her look especially short and chubby. Maybe it wasn't a bad thing she was missing breakfast.

"You'd better hurry up then," said Dave, returning his comb to his bag and fastening it. "See you later." He shouldered the bag and left. As the door closed behind him, Carrie looked at her reflection in the mirror, checking for any spots that might have appeared overnight. She leaned in to peer at a suspicious white dot on her chin. As she did so her image disappeared, and a message replaced it. The mirror wasn't only a mirror, it was a communication screen. The message it was displaying was the results of the deep brain scan the Council had performed on the two of them overnight.

Carrie's hands fell away from her face as she read the figures. Their levels of ability were shown as percentages, and Carrie's and Dave's were very different, but not in the way Carrie would have expected. Dave's compatibility with the role of Transgalactic Council Liaison Officer was ninety-seven per cent. Hers was thirty-four. Thirty-four.

She gripped the sides of her locker. How could it be possible? She had always known that her selection for the Officer role had been a fluke. She had happened to write an ad on a dating website that was the exact code for the job application, and because she loved the Officer's bag she had strong-armed Gavin into taking her on. But she had always assumed, deep down, that she could do the work. Hadn't she been the one to uncover the placktoids' lies and their blackmailing of the squashpumps? None of the others had seen what she had, not even oh-so-perfect Belinda. And hadn't she discovered that the placktoids were in league with the dandrobians, former tyrants of the galaxy?

Could it be true that she was terrible at the job, and that level-headed Dave would be much better? She swallowed as she thought of the week ahead, imagining her friend, who she had taken such pains to persuade to come along, beating her at every exercise. She imagined the final decision by the Council to fire her and hire Dave instead. And he didn't even want the job.

The results glared out at her from the screen. She couldn't let Dave see them. It was just too embarrassing. She waved a hand over it and breathed a sigh of relief as the message disappeared.

***

Her friend looked at her quizzically as she entered the training room. Guessing her misery must be written all over her face, she faked a smile and went to the opposite end of the line of trainees. She could avoid difficult questions until break time at least, and hopefully by then she would have got over her shock and could act more normal. The room was empty. Carrie wondered what today's training was. She hadn't had time to read her briefing device.

The other trainees ranged out between her and Dave, all variously attired in bright orange. The large green blob, who had introduced herself at dinner as Audrey, got about by rolling, and seemed almost entirely encased in fabric. For some reason the faceless hairy creature only had a narrow circlet of orange around its head. The box the oootoon lived in had been painted orange.

Errruorerrrrrhch was leading the session. "Welcome...at last," said the alien to Carrie as she took her place. "As I was just explaining, due to the current pan-galactic crisis, we have decided to include additional elements in our Officer equipment and training. Customarily, Council staff are unarmed. Our roles are diplomatic and the possession of weapons is contrary to our aims of administration, coordination, management and reconciliation. In the present climate, however, Officer safety is our primary concern. Unity and Council staff are stretched thin across the galaxy as we attempt to locate the placktoids and protect galactic citizens, and it is possible you may find yourselves alone and in danger."

Weapons. Cool, thought Carrie. Images of scifi skirmishes on TV and film, with phasers, laser guns and other futuristic arms, came into her mind. *But how will we fit them in our bags?*

"We are also faced with the problem that placktoid exoskeletons are notoriously strong and tough, and the most powerful weaponry penetrates them poorly, even at close range. The latest weapon designs are, we believe, more effective, though of course we have no placktoids to test them on, were such an endeavour even ethical," the insectoid alien paused before adding, "which it is not."

Carrie sighed. When was she going to stop waffling and give them their guns?

"This morning you will practice using the new equipment, but once training is over, all weapons must be returned. It is strictly prohibited to carry these or any other arms aboard a Council starship."

Duh! Come on, hurry up. Glancing at the squashpump beside her, Carrie wondered how on Earth it was going to carry a massive laser cannon.

"Now, please collect a weapon. I will explain how to use them before we begin."

Carrie looked around the room. Where was the gun cabinet? Or big box of arms? Then she saw it. At Errruorerrrrrhch's feet, or rather, her front claws, was a square hole. A small, square hole. Elbowing the other trainees aside, she went to it, squatted down and looked in. The hole was full of small green objects about the size of cigarette lighters. She sat back on her heels. *These are the weapons?* She picked one up. It was smooth and rectangular. There was no trigger nor even a button to press.

"I apologise, Officer Hatchett," said Errruorerrrrrhch. "In the haste to design and manufacture these weapons, we were unable to include the usual attachments for human use. Hopefully, during this session both you and the other human can learn to use thought operation."

"Tsk. They canna work things w' their minds?" said the squashpump. It had jumped into the hole and was holding a weapon with its tentacles.

"Don't be rude," said the oootoon, as Errruorerrrrrhch dropped a weapon into it. The green object sank beneath the yellow liquid before bobbing to the surface. "They can't help it. Humans are very nice. One day they'll catch up. Yes, one day. No need to point out their weaknesses."

"Och, you're right. Sorry aboot that."

"That's okay," said Carrie. Dave tried to catch her eye as he collected a weapon, but she looked away.

Errruorerrrrrhch explained that the trainees would practise shooting holograms of the various placktoid types until break time. The weapons were set to practice mode so they were harmless, but she warned the humans to take care they didn't accidentally change the settings to operational.

Crap, Carrie thought, *how am I supposed to tell?*

"Simply point the weapon at the target, concentrate hard, and will it to fire," Errruorerrrrrhch advised her and Dave.

When holographic placktoids appeared before

them, all the trainees except the humans fired their weapons simultaneously, and the placktoids they hit blinked out. Carrie pointed her weapon at a stapler placktoid and willed it to fire with all her might, but nothing happened. She was secretly pleased to see Dave also fail. It was one thing at least he didn't do better than her.

But on the next try, Dave's weapon sputtered to life and a bright beam shone out, while Carrie drew another blank. He didn't hit a placktoid, but he had done better than her. He looked over at her, grinning. Carrie returned a half-hearted smile, and frowned with concentration as another set of placktoids appeared. This time they were moving, though slowly. Again, she failed to fire her weapon. Dave not only fired, he hit a placktoid. He whooped, and Audrey bumped into him in what Carrie supposed was a gesture of congratulations.

By break time, Carrie had, with a huge effort of concentration, managed to fire her weapon once, and at the time she had been pointing it at Errruorerrrrhch, who had performed an impressive feat of gymnastics in leaping right across the room.

"Don't worry, you'll get there." said Dave as they forced down a drink that was pretending to be coffee, though it actually tasted like a throat infection Carrie had contracted when she was nine.

It might have been her imagination, but she was sure she detected a patronising tone in her friend's voice.

CHAPTER EIGHT – DECISIONS, DECISIONS

"You will be given further opportunities to practise using the new weapons at regular intervals during your training," said Errruorerrrrrhch as they lined up for the afternoon session. Carrie's heart sank. Her skills at controlling a gun with her mind hadn't improved much after the morning break. She had always known her powers of concentration weren't good, but being beaten by a box of custard was pretty demoralising. Dave's prowess had improved with each shot he took.

Oh well, Carrie thought, *maybe this session will be about something I'm good at.*

"This afternoon we will be concentrating on logical thought processes and effective decision-making."

Carrie's shoulders slumped. The door opened, and a robot cart carrying an assortment of helmets entered. The two that looked as though they were for Carrie and Dave had opaque visors similar to those on Unity helmets. Errruorerrrrrhch instructed the trainees to put on their helmets. Carrie wondered how the oootoon would put on a helmet, but when she looked around she couldn't see its box. She put up a hand. "Shouldn't we wait for everyone to arrive?"

"All the required trainees are present," replied Errruorerrrrhch. "Where a session has little benefit to a candidate, it does not appear on the individual's schedule. During this free time the trainee is expected to practise other skills. This information was stated in your itinerary on your briefing device."

Oh, that, thought Carrie. She would have to have a look at it that evening after dinner. She closed the visor on her helmet and a vision of a landscape appeared before her eyes. A familiar landscape. The legend at the bottom of the screen read:

> THESE SCENARIOS ARE DRAWN
> FROM REAL-LIFE TRANSGALACTIC
> INTERCULTURAL COMMUNITY
> CRISIS LIAISON OFFICERS'
> EXPERIENCES. AT THE CRUCIAL
> DECISION POINT THE SCENE WILL
> FREEZE AND YOU WILL BE
> OFFERED SEVERAL OPTIONS. YOUR
> FINAL DECISION WILL BE
> RECORDED BY YOUR DEVICE. THE
> PROBLEMS INCREASE IN
> DIFFICULTY.

Carrie sat on the floor and crossed her legs as the video began to play. She was back in Dandrobia, at her first meeting with the dandrobians and squashpumps. The events played out exactly as she remembered them. A gust of wind blew, toppling the squashpump Foreign Secretary's column, which sliced him in two. The squashpumps began leaping onto dandrobian heads and invading their brains in revenge. Apate, the ebony-haired dandrobian, appeared from behind Carrie's seat, wringing her hands and telling Carrie she must leave right away before the rest of the squashpumps arrived. The screen froze and words appeared.

SHOULD YOU:

A) IMMEDIATELY CONTACT YOUR MANAGER TO OPEN A TRANSGALACTIC GATEWAY

B) REMAIN DURING THE HOSTILITIES IN ORDER TO ASSESS THE SITUATION FURTHER

C) PUT A SAFE DISTANCE BETWEEN YOURSELF AND THE UNHARMED DANDROBIAN BEFORE CONTACTING YOUR MANAGER AND REQUESTING A TRANSGALACTIC GATEWAY

D) NONE OF THE ABOVE. PLEASE INSERT YOUR ANSWER

Carrie's face burned. She wondered whether the other trainees knew this had happened to her. Dave certainly did. Now that she saw the options in black and white, the right decision seemed obvious, but she decided to submit the decision she made at the time anyway. The Council hadn't been there. They didn't know what it had been like when she was in the middle of it all. She concentrated and thought the letter

A.

> WRONG. THE CORRECT ANSWER IS
> C. IF YOU GAVE AN UNLISTED
> ANSWER A RESPONSE WILL BE
> SENT TO YOUR CABIN
> COMMUNICATION DEVICE THIS
> EVENING.

As the next scenario appeared, Carrie's heart sank further. Now she was back on the placktoid starship after her first encounter with the placktoid commander. She was lifted into the giant paperclip and returned to the oootoon planet surface, where the paperclip dumped her in the yellow oootoon ocean. When she had made it to shore, the screen froze.

SHOULD YOU:

A) COMMUNICATE WITH THE
OOOTOON USING YOUR
TRANSLATOR AND ATTEMPT TO
FIND OUT WHAT HAS HAPPENED
TO THE MISSING PLACKTOIDS.

B) CONTACT YOUR MANAGER FOR
INSTRUCTIONS

C) EAT SOME OF THE OOOTOON
(THIS IS A SERIOUS OPTION)

D) NONE OF THE ABOVE. PLEASE
INSERT YOUR ANSWER

Carrie cringed and thanked her lucky stars the box of oootoon wasn't at the session. This time even she couldn't justify her actions. She thought the letter A. The screen flashed CORRECT WELL DONE before moving on to another sequence of events.

By the end of the afternoon her head was buzzing with decision-making. She hadn't thought it was possible for your brain to actually hurt with thinking. For all her effort, she only managed to score seventy-five per cent correct. As she removed her helmet, she caught sight of Dave's face. He was smiling, and when he noticed her looking at him, he gave her a thumbs up. She smiled back weakly.

As they returned to their cabin to freshen up before dinner, her friend chattered about how much fun the afternoon had been. Carrie said little, and when her friend told her he had scored ninety-one, she congratulated him without reporting her own result.

They hadn't gone far before Errruorerrrrrhch caught up with them. Carrie was grateful for the distraction until the alien said, "I hope you were not excessively dismayed by the Council's use of your own experiences as an Officer in our training material. It is standard practice. We have found that trainees benefit most from observing real-life experiences in the field."

"Oh no, I don't mind at all," replied Carrie through her teeth. Dave looked away.

"Good. It is always preferable to accept our errors and learn from them. Do you not agree?"

"Yes, I...hello, Gavin." Her former manager had appeared around a bend in the corridor, covered in his children. As soon as he spotted them, however, he about-faced and sped away. "Wow, what's up with him?"

Errruorerrrrrhch chittered. "He is fearful of me. It is very tiresome. In our species, the mother is occasionally driven to eat the weaker of her offspring. It was for this reason it became the custom for the father to care for them during the earliest stage, when they appear the most tasty. Of course, I would never dream of ingesting the little...morsels. Their father is excessively cautious."

Dave stumbled and fell against the wall, where he remained as Carrie and Errruorerrrrrhch walked on. Carrie swallowed. "It seems a bit weird he's here, then. I mean, if he's so paranoid that you'll eat your kids."

"Your words surprise me, Officer Hatchett. You are apparently unaware that your manager has a special attachment to you. His philandering habits were about to result in his third and final dismissal from a Transgalactic Council position when you uncovered the placktoid plot, thereby winning him a reprieve. He believes you have a fresh and original approach to your role. He is here to watch over your progress as he does not wish to lose you from his team. From the discussions we have had regarding your performance, I believe it would not be excessive for me to say that he cares about you."

Her vision suddenly blurring, all Carrie could say was, "Really?"

***

The news that Gavin was there for her had eased Carrie's mind a little by the time she got back to the cabin with Dave. Maybe she could go to him for tips on what to do to get through the week and pass the course.

The clothing that had been placed on their bunks in readiness for the next day's training also made her feel better. At last, here was something she had a chance of succeeding in. Something she knew she could do much better than Dave. On her bed was a fluorescent orange swimsuit, and on Dave's were swimming trunks.

Her friend blinked several times. "But I can't swim."

CHAPTER NINE – INTO THE DEEP

Carrie dived eagerly into the clear water of the Council starship swimming pool the following day. She swam to the far end of the pool, flipped, pushed away with her feet, and swam back again. Dave stood at the edge, his arms hanging at his sides. Propping her elbows on the pool wall, Carrie looked up at her friend. "Jump in," she said. "It's shallow at this end. Look." She stood on the bottom to show him that the water only came up to her shoulders.

Dave sat down and slid carefully into the water. He shivered and gripped his upper arms. "It's freezing."

"No it isn't. Splash about a bit to warm yourself up."

He patted the water like it was a friendly dog. Carrie turned her head to hide a smile.

"I don't know why they've included swimming in the training," said Dave. "It isn't like we'd ever use it."

Noting her friend's use of 'we', as if finally imagining himself as a Liaison Officer, Carrie replied, "Of course we could. Remember when we got thrown in the oootoon ocean? If you'd been able to swim you wouldn't have panicked so much."

"I didn't panic."

"Yes, you did. I told you to keep still, but you were flailing about like a fish on speed."

Dave's mouth lifted at a corner. "Well, maybe a little. So would you if you thought you were going to die."

A massive invertebrate Neptune rose up out of the water between them. Errruorerrrrrhch had arrived. Dave said, "Bloody hell," and left the pool in a blur of movement. Carrie and the rest of the trainees remained in the water, bobbing around. To Carrie's eyes, Audrey looked most at home, closely followed by the oootoon, which had oozed out of its box and was expanding into long, thick, yellow ribbons as if enjoying its escape from confinement.

"The first half of this morning's session is devoted to becoming accustomed to moving in a liquid," said Errruorerrrrrhch. "Several galactic civilisations are aquatic, as I'm sure you are aware, and while some of you are very familiar with this environment, others may need some practice at effective locomotion. You are expected to maintain your swimming skills through regular training for the duration of your employment."

Audrey bumped lazily into Carrie and she pushed her away, giggling. This session was going to be fun.

"After break you will perform underwater

tasks," said Errruorerrrrrhch. "These tasks assess your physical agility and strength. Neither skill is essential for the performance of your duties, but they may at times prove useful in the diverse situations an Officer experiences."

Errruorerrrrrhch continued speaking, but Carrie was already idly swimming across the pool. She had heard all the important stuff. When she returned, Errruorerrrrrhch had left and Dave was in the pool again. He was standing in the corner looking cold while the other trainees were frolicking around him. Carrie couldn't help but feel a small, guilty surge of pleasure at his predicament. But he was still her friend, and it was she who had persuaded him to attend the training. She swam up to him. "Come on, I'll help you."

Her friend shook his head. "There's no point. I'll never learn to swim in a single morning. I thought I'd try, but I don't know what to do. I might as well get out and tell Errruorerrrrrhch I can't do it."

"Don't give up before you've started. Learning to swim is really important, even if you don't work for the Transgalactic Council. Come over here with me." Dave followed her out into deeper water. "Now, hold my hands, and start kicking with your feet." She gripped his hands as he lifted his feet off the floor and began to move them. "Wait, hold on." She tightened her grip. "Okay, try again." Once more he kicked. "Erm...could you stop for a minute?" As her friend stood on the pool floor, she looked down at his legs and feet. "How are you doing it?"

"Doing what?"

"How are you kicking? You're going backwards."

"No I'm not."

"Yes, you are. You're pulling me towards you. You should be pushing me away."

Dave sighed. "It's no good. I can't do it."

"Yes, you can. Let's try again."

"Okay, if you like. But it's a waste of time."

Carrie grabbed Dave's hands and pulled him gently forward as he kicked. She also helped him practise trying to float, and taught him the movements for breaststroke and front crawl. She couldn't remember learning to swim and had always been a natural in the water, so she wasn't sure if she was teaching Dave the right way, but after half an hour or so he managed a few strokes.

"Brilliant," she exclaimed. "Well done."

Dave wiped water from his face. "Thanks," he said, "but I don't think I'll be winning any championships just yet."

"We all have to start somewhere." The other trainees were getting out of the water. "It must be nearly break time."

"Yeah. I think I'll ask Errruorerrrrrhch if I can skip the second half. I'm never going to be able to do underwater stuff."

"You never know until you try." Carrie actually thought Dave was probably right, but she wanted to be encouraging. As she pulled herself up onto the side, however, the sight that greeted her made her wonder if Dave might be able to join in after all. In a corner of the swimming area was a pile of bright orange wetsuits.

***

While the trainees were getting ready for the second session, a mechanical, grinding sound came from the pool. The floor was sliding back, revealing a lower level much deeper than the first. Dave was looking pale. "Don't worry," said Carrie, "it looks like we'll be diving. You don't have to worry about sinking because you're already underwater. But where's our scuba gear?" Carrie lifted up a helmet. It had an elongated snout, like a dog's muzzle. There was no sign of any masks or gas cylinders.

"If you are unable to breathe in water, place your respiration tablets in the receptacle in your helmets, and check that you can breathe normally before entering the pool," said Errruorerrrrrhch.

Respiration tablets? Carrie frowned. What did the Manager mean? Most of the other trainees were slipping directly into the water without the need for any artificial breathing device. Dave was searching through his Liaison Officer's toolbox.

"Is this it?" He held up the item that Carrie had thought looked like a dishwasher tablet. The item that she had opened and broken.

"Yes," said Errruorerrrrrhch. "Take it out of its wrapper and place it in the receptacle in your helmet. The tablet supplies your oxygen needs and removes carbon dioxide from the gases you exhale."

Dave looked sidelong at Carrie's forlorn face. "Actually," he said to Errruorerrrrhch. "Is it okay if I sit this out? I'm a terrible swimmer." He passed his unopened tablet to Carrie.

Carrie sighed as she pushed his hand away. She couldn't let her friend cover up for her stupid mistakes, and she didn't want him to give up on learning to swim.

"Errruorerrrrh, I don't have my respirator tablet. I opened it earlier. I'm sorry."

The alien chittered. "I will request another from Supplies. Please wait for it to be delivered."

"Honestly, Carrie, you can have mine," said Dave as Errruorerrrrhch left. "I've had enough for today. I don't want to get in there again, especially not to go diving."

Pulling on her wetsuit, Carrie replied, "Look, you did so well in the first session. Don't stop now. Learning to swim is actually harder than diving. When you're swimming, you have to use your arms and legs at the same time. Under water you just kick your legs to move around. No strokes or anything like that."

Dave grimaced as he peered at the trainees who were sinking to the bottom of the pool. Carrie looked down too. There seemed to be an obstacle course down there. "I don't know," said Dave. "I've never done anything like this before."

"Then now's a good time to start," said Carrie

brightly. "Come on, you've actually enjoyed yourself a bit so far, haven't you?"

Her friend nodded. "It's been a lot more fun than I thought it would be."

Probably because you're ninety-seven per cent suited to being a Liaison Officer, thought Carrie. A small robot carrier bearing a respirator tablet appeared at her side.

"Okay, I'll give it a try."

Carrie smiled at her friend, her face tight.

CHAPTER TEN – FALLING OUT

Carrie swung her legs over the side of the top bunk and stretched pleasantly. She was sleeping well on the Council starship and had no worries about her dog, Rogue, or her cat, Toodles, missing her while she was away. When the Council sent her home via transgalactic gateway only a minute or two would have passed on Earth. Dave was already dressed and was combing his hair. The dirty clothes and other bits and bobs she had left on the floor had been mysteriously put away overnight.

"So, what are we doing today?" she asked.

Dave tutted. "Don't tell me you still haven't read the itinerary. We've been here four days."

"I did read it. I've just forgotten," Carrie lied. She'd intended to read the itinerary. She just hadn't got around to it yet.

Checking his face for stubble, her friend said, "All it says for today is 'practical training'."

She jumped down with a thump. "I wonder what that is. Seems like most things we've done so far have been practical. Maybe I can ask Gavin at breakfast if he's there. I haven't seen him recently." Carrie bent down to pick up a small green object that had fallen from underneath Dave's bunk when she jumped.

"He's got his work cut out with his nightmare kids, I should think," said Dave. "That and preventing their mother from snacking on them at break." He shuddered.

"What's this?" Carrie gasped and turned, wide-eyed, to her friend. In her hand was the small green object. It was one of the weapons they had trained with.

Dave looked away quickly. "Wow, where did that come from?"

"Dave," Carrie exclaimed. "you know full well where it came from. It just fell from your bed. When did you take it? When we were training?"

"Well, thanks a lot for jumping to conclusions! You don't know I took it."

"You do have a bit of history of that kind of thing, you know. And how would it get here otherwise? Why on Earth did you take a weapon? They're incredibly dangerous. You'll have to give it back."

"Not if I didn't take it," replied her friend, his nostrils flaring.

"Of course you did. Stop playing games. You could get me into trouble too. Did you think about that?" Carrie exclaimed, her heart racing at the realisation that her friend had put her job at risk.

"Well, of all the cheek. Just because I have a medical condition I'm suddenly responsible for stealing every random item you come across." He put his hands on his hips. "I'm only here because of you. I've been to all the training exercises, even spending hours in a freezing swimming pool. I've put up with your disgusting habits all week—"

"DISGUSTING."

"Yes, disgusting. Strands of hair left in the sink, yesterday's clothes lying on the floor, rubbish scattered about. In all the times I've visited you at home, Carrie, I never said anything about your flat. Your place, your rules, I thought. But I'm telling you now that, frankly, it's awful. I know you have pets, but that's no excuse."

"How dare you. I might be a little messy, but I am NOT disgusting. And at least I don't have OCD. Arranging all my possessions in a neat little pattern every night." She screwed up her eyes and nose as she mimicked placing objects on a surface. "Everything in EXACTLY the same place. Honestly, Dave, you'll make some man a lovely HOUSEKEEPER someday. AND I've noticed your disgust doesn't stop you from eating me out of house and home whenever you're over. Biscuits don't grow on trees you know."

Dave's eyes widened and his mouth formed an O. "IF I ate all your biscuits, which I DON'T, I'd be doing you a favour," he exclaimed. "You could do WITHOUT eating so many biscuits if you ask me." He poked her in the belly.

Carrie drew in a great breath of air, ready to explode with indignation. But her outrage was so great she couldn't speak. Her mouth worked, but the words wouldn't come, and she stood rigid, glaring at Dave with her hands clenched and her mouth wide open.

Dave glared back at her. "Yes? Was there something you wanted to say?"

Still words couldn't convey Carrie's ire, and she closed and opened her mouth like a fish out of water. She looked so comical, Dave's anger melted and his lips twitched as he tried to prevent a smile. Seeing this, a great snort of laughter burst from Carrie, and she grabbed her mouth. Her friend also began to chuckle, and soon guffaws gripped them both until they were weeping with mirth. They clung to each other as they laughed.

Finally Carrie caught her breath enough to speak. She wiped her eyes as she said, "Seriously, though, what are you going to do with it? You can't keep it here."

Sighing, Dave replied, "I don't know. What do you think I should do?"

Carrie sat down on his bed and turned the weapon over in her hands. "It is an amazing thing, isn't it? So small, and yet powerful enough to penetrate a placktoid." Dave sat beside her. Carrie looked at him from the corners of her eyes. "You haven't taken anything else, have you?"

"Of course not," he exclaimed. When Carrie's eyes didn't move, his facial muscles relaxed. "I haven't, honestly."

"The thing is, I don't understand," she said. "You're such a together person. You're so level-headed and sensible. You don't seem to have any baggage or problems. People with kleptomania are messed up in some way, as far as I understand it."

Dave shrugged. "I don't know that I really have kleptomania. I've never been diagnosed. I just find certain things irresistibly fascinating. Neat, complex, clever things, you know? And there's a challenge to it—taking things without anyone noticing, I mean. It's such a thrill to succeed. I don't thing it's such a bad thing to do. I never keep anything for long. I always put back whatever I've taken, eventually."

Carrie watched her friend closely as he spoke. This was a side to him she had never seen. When he stopped she smiled and gave him a sideways shove with her shoulder. "There's a lot more to you than meets the eye, isn't there? I wonder what Gavin would have to say if he knew you were a closet thrill-seeker. You're supposed to be the one who keeps me grounded."

"I am sensible most of the time." He took the weapon from her hand. "Not sure what I'm going to do now, though. I suppose I'll have to 'fess up. I doubt I'll be able to put it back without being seen. And it wouldn't be right to take it back home with me."

"Don't tell them. You'll get kicked off the programme." Carrie frowned. "I know. Leave it somewhere. Somewhere it'll be found quickly."

"That's no good. They'll know someone stole it, and they'll test the DNA on it and find out it was me. I don't know how to clean it to make sure there's no trace of anything left."

"Doesn't matter. Your DNA—and mine, now—your DNA being on it doesn't prove anything. We were all taking weapons out of that store. All the weapons have trainees' DNA on them."

Putting his hand slowly to his chin, Dave nodded. "Maybe you're right. Okay, it's worth a try. Maybe I could find a place in the canteen or another communal room where I can put it." He stood.

"Do it now, before we go to the practical training session."

But her friend was looking away from the door and towards a wall. "Too late. Look at that. I thought it was only a mirror." He was looking at the communication screen. Carrie leaned out from the bunk to read the message.

ARRIVED AT GAGINION. REPORT TO
THE LEVEL 2 CENTRAL AIRLOCK
FOR PRACTICAL TRAINING.

She leaped up. "We're on a planet. That's what they meant by practical training."

"Of course," said Dave. "The itinerary didn't go into any detail."

"All this time we thought we were just floating in space, we've been travelling somewhere," Carrie exclaimed. "I wonder what it looks like." She ran to the cabin window and ripped off the T-shirt Dave had hung over it. The sight that greeted her made her stagger back. Beyond the starship was not the alien landscape she had expected.

Slowly, she returned to the window and

pressed her face against the surface, flattening her nose. She gazed out into an aquatic, shadowy expanse. Pale green, rippling light came from above, lighting the area around the ship for a short distance. Beyond was darkness, where Carrie could make out only vague, moving shapes. She looked down into black, seemingly bottomless depths.

"Bloody hell," said Dave.

CHAPTER ELEVEN – CARRIE'S OFF

"Gaginion is home to seventeen sentient species," Errruorerrrrrhch explained to the trainees waiting at the airlock, wearing wetsuits or only their Transgalactic Liaison Officer swimsuits as appropriate to their species. Carrie and Dave, as humans, needed the protection of wetsuits against the chill water. "The predominant species, marsoliie, have divided into two factions, Singles and Groups. The Singles have applied to the Council for mediation with the Group marsoliie—"

"The same species?" asked Carrie.

"Yes, the same species. The information is on your briefing device. We were uncertain whether we would be able to provide this training until very recently, and we uploaded the necessary details only this morning. Please take a moment to read through all the information before leaving on your assignment. You have plenty of time. But to give you an overview, Group marsoliie believe their species is most successful, happy and fulfilled when conjoined with others of their species, in groups of indiscriminate numbers. The Groups believe they evolved to exist together once they have reached maturity, and that living as a Single once adulthood is attained is an unnatural, abhorrent and unhealthy practice.

"Single marsoliie, as is often the case in intracultural disputes, believes the exact opposite: that living as a Single organism is the normal and natural state of affairs—"

"Can't they just live and let live?" Carrie asked. "I mean, the Singles live alone and the Groups join up?"

A pause followed this second interruption, and the trainees turned to look at Carrie.

"IF I could explain," continued Errruorerrrrrhch, "the central problem seems to reside in the fact that the Group marsoliie feel they must *help* the Single marsoliie to a better life by capturing them and adding them to their number. This physical coercion is obviously illegal, but it is very difficult to prove. Once a Single's neural network is joined to the Group, it retains no memory of itself as a Single, but instead it remembers, thinks and feels as one of the Group."

"Oh, I see," said Carrie.

Errruorerrrrrhch turned her giant insect head towards her, waited a moment, and continued. "Though the marsoliie have achieved interstellar travel, they employ little technology in their day-to-day lives. Neither do they have any centralised government nor legal system. Disputes are resolved on a case-by-case basis within communities. These small, local disputes are happening across the planet. Though serious, the Council does not currently have the staff numbers to address the issue. Therefore, we deemed this liaison request as an appropriate practical training exercise for new Officers.

"Your assignment is essentially to attend community talks between the Singles and Groups and ensure there is fair play. A further reason we have chosen this assignment for you is that the Unity soldiers who are currently doing all they can to protect the Single marsoliie from assimilation are spread extremely thin, due to the placktoid threat. Your presence should be a further deterrent."

Carrie opened her mouth, but decided against speaking, and closed it again.

"A plentiful supply of respirator tablets is available for those who need them. I repeat, please read your briefing documents thoroughly before leaving the ship and travelling to the coordinates programmed into your briefing device. Underwater scramblers are available outside the airlock."

"What are they?" asked Carrie. "Like aquatic motorbikes or something?"

"I believe you could say so," answered Errruorerrrrrhch.

"Cool," exclaimed Carrie. She had put on only the lower half of her wetsuit. The upper half hung down from her hips. She pulled it up and slipped her arms into the sleeves. "Hey, if we run out of respirator tablets, it isn't that much of a problem, is it? I mean, we can just swim up to the surface, right?"

"Gaginion's atmosphere is composed almost entirely of carbon dioxide. I do not think it would offer a human much benefit if you were attempt to breathe it."

"Oh...okay." Carrie zipped the wetsuit up to her chin and picked up her helmet.

"Don't you think you should read the briefing first?" asked Dave.

"No, it's fine. Errruorerrrrrhch told us the important parts, and I can read the rest on the way." She put on her helmet and picked up her fins. Dave reached over, pulled the helmet off her head and put it down on the floor.

"Carrie, read the briefing document."

"Hey...oh...fine." Putting down her fins, she pulled the tablet of clear plastic out of her Liaison Officer toolbox, thumbed it until she reached the correct screen and hastily scanned the text. The other trainees milled around, getting ready to leave. Carrie paged ahead to images of the marsoliie. The briefing device played a video of a bright scarlet creature moving through water. It looked similar to a starfish except that it had eight legs, and they were frilled and flexible. The animal swam by undulating its legs and body, and it travelled in a delicate, pulsating flurry of movement. "Wow, amazing." As Carrie watched, a set of joined marsoliie appeared. The Group was a large ball of billowing legs. It approached the Single, grabbing one its legs with several of its own. After drawing the Single close, it attached the centre of its body to its mass. The conjoined animals then beat their legs as one and disappeared out of the frame. Carrie nodded. "I see."

She picked up her helmet and fins and grabbed a handful of respirator tablets, which she shoved into her Liaison Officer toolbox. She said a quick goodbye to Dave and, banging her fist on the airlock door, she called, "Open up." A scent of salty gardenias came from the translator in her toolbox, and the door hissed open. She stepped inside, and Audrey rolled in with her. Like everything else that Audrey carried, her toolbox was somewhere inside her. Her huge wetsuit covered most of her body. A portion of green poked through a hole, and, for Carrie's benefit, Audrey formed it into a human-like head and gave Carrie a smile.

The other trainees were still reading their briefing devices and getting ready. Carrie didn't want to wait, so she told the door to close. "Good luck," she said to Audrey. She burped in reply, which Carrie's translated relayed to her mind as "Thanks, you too."

"Wait a moment, please, Carrie," said a familiar voice. Gavin and his children had appeared. The airlock door was closing.

"Sorry, I'm going on an assignment," Carrie said. "No time to talk."

"I wanted to inform you—"

"I'll see you when I get back." The airlock door closed, shutting out the light from the corridor. Only the pale air lock light and the watery green beams through the window illuminated the space. Water began to enter the chamber from vents in the outer door. Carrie put on her fins and helmet, ripped open a respirator tablet and popped it into the receptacle in front of her mouth and nose. The water had risen to her knees. Audrey floated on the surface, bobbing gently. Carrie pulled her bag's strap over her head and zipped it closed. She wasn't going to risk all her useful devices disappearing into the ocean.

She grinned at Audrey, who bumped her in return. The water rose higher until she, too, was floating. She dipped her head beneath the surface, breathing deeply as she did so. Her respirator tablet was working, and the indicator was way over to the left, which meant it was at maximum capacity. When the needle reached the centre she was supposed to exchange the tablet for another, though she wouldn't be in any danger of oxygen starvation until the needle swung far to the right.

At last the water reached the top of the airlock and Carrie and Audrey were entirely submerged. The outer door began to open. As soon as there was room for her, Carrie slipped beneath it, giving Audrey a wave. Outside the starship, she stopped a moment to take stock of her surroundings. Though mysterious depths sank away beneath her and watery shadows encircled, excitement surged through her at finally being free of the confines of the starship.

She spun to locate the aquatic motorbikes. As Errruorerrrrrhch had said, they were tethered to the starship, floating in a line. The underwater scooters were in a range of sizes and shapes. Two of them looked as though they were made for humans, and Carrie swam to the nearest one and strapped herself in. Her heart was racing. After far too many days of boring training, she was finally off to do her job.

Cautiously, she opened her bag and fished inside. She pulled out the briefing device and slotted it into a frame on the water scooter dashboard. Coordinates flashed. She gripped the machine's handles and rotated the right grip. It sprang forward, but stopped. Carrie looked back to see what the problem was. Her scooter was dragging at the others that were tethered to the line. Audrey, who had just boarded hers, had been bounced off and was floating away.

"Sorry," called Carrie as she released her scooter from its tether. She was off, zooming through the water.

CHAPTER TWELVE – STRANGE ENCOUNTERS

On her way to the meeting of Single and Group marsoliie, Carrie encountered other creatures living in the ocean. For a while her water scooter carried her underneath a large mass that she assumed was a raft of seaweed or another non-intelligent substance—until the mass began to shift and she heard a voice that sounded like the tinkling of bells. "You're one of those Transgalactic Council Officers, aren't you. Aren't you going to introduce yourself?"

Carrie stopped her scooter. All around nothing else was visible but the slowly moving raft above her. She looked up at the dark vegetation. "Sorry, I didn't notice...I mean, I didn't think...I mean, sorry. Hello."

"You're here to stop the those marsoliie fighting, I assume? A good thing, too. They should all stay as Singles. A large Group gets in the way. Can't go over it, can't go under it. Have to go round it. Everyone would be much better off if they were all Singles."

"We're going to do what we can," replied Carrie, wondering how big the Groups could grow if they got in the way of the monster above her. "I'm here to oversee a mediation meeting.

But resources are stretched because of the problem with the placktoids."

"I heard about that," said the Thing above. "I'd like to see them try to come here. I'd soon deal with them."

I'm sure you would, thought Carrie, gazing into the dark, amorphous shape. The green light of the alien sun filtered through the water at the edge of it, in the distance. "Well, it's been nice meeting you, but I really must get on." She started her scooter and whizzed forward.

A distance meter was ticking down on her display. According to the meter, she had nearly arrived at the meeting place, though she couldn't yet see any sign of the marsoliie. She wondered what their dwellings looked like. This area of the ocean was quite shallow, and she had seen apparently artificial shapes below, but she didn't know if they belonged to the marsoliie or another of the planet's sentient species. Or even if they were constructed and not natural.

As she looked up, she spotted a mass of scarlet ahead. The right side of the mass was much larger than the left, which looked thin and wispy in comparison. As she drew closer the mass became more defined. To the right were large Groups of marsoliie, all their many legs writhing in a frilled throng. To the left were Singles, which were pulsating and flowing and floating in a beautiful sychronised dance.

Carrie slowed her scooter to get a better look at the Singles. A deep, smooth tenor voice sounded in her head, growing louder as she approached. It was announcing the beginning of the meeting, "as the Transgalactic Council Officer has arrived."

Floating forward on the last of her scooter's momentum, Carrie was nearly among the marsoliie before a sudden realisation struck her: how was she supposed to speak to these aliens? Would they hear her through her helmet? Probably not. Did they use telepathy to talk to each other? Gavin had told her once that humans weren't very telepathic. She frowned. Had there been something about communication media in the briefing document? Maybe she had skipped that part. She would just have to try her best.

She clipped her scooter's tether to her belt and kicked her fins to bring her the last few metres to the waiting marsoliie. "Hi." As she spoke, her right arm flipped up. Carrie blinked. She pulled her arm down. "I'm Transgalactic Intercultural Community Crisis Liaison Officer Hatch—oh my goodness." Her arms had flown up, gesticulating wildly, and her body twisted round. At the same time her knees moved akimbo and both her legs kicked out. By the time the word 'goodness' was out of her mouth, she was upside down and facing away from the watching aliens.

Carrie caught her breath as she tried to understand what was happening. She spun round and turned herself right side up. "I—" Her head flew back. "Would like—" She shimmied. "To—" Her hips ground. "Apologise for my behaviour." She finished in a rush while she pirouetted, shuddered and turned a cartwheel.

"I'm not sure I understand you," replied the Single marsoliie, undulating as his voice sounded in Carrie's mind. "You have nothing to apologise for. Shall we start the meeting?"

Her body rigid, Carrie whispered, "Yes." As the word left her lips, she gave the marsoliie the finger. With both hands. She gripped her arms to her chest. What was going on?

The marsoliie were motionless except for the Single who had apparently spoken. He began to billow and ripple in an elegant frolic. "We would like to begin the meeting by thanking our neighbourhood Groups for coming," he said. "We hope we can resolve our differences amicably and to everyone's satisfaction."

Light began to dawn in Carrie's mind. The marsoliie communicated through body language. Whenever she spoke her translator prompted her body to move, conveying the meaning of her words to the marsoliie. With her new understanding, her heart slowed. She hadn't been incredibly rude. In the marsoliie's eyes—or whatever it was they saw with—she'd been acting normally. She exhaled with relief. She couldn't afford to mess this up, what with her being on *remedial training*. Her lips tightened.

A Group marsoliie began to move its legs in delicate synchronisation. "We certainly hope so too. We'd like to take the opportunity to explain our position and clear up any misunderstandings you may have."

"Well, we're happy to listen to whatever you have to say," replied the Single. "So, let's each start by stating our viewpoints. Would you like to go first?"

"Thank you," said the Group. "I'd like to begin by making it clear we are only acting according to the facts stated in the *Natural Lives of Marsoliie*."

A Single to one side shivered, and Carrie heard, "You can hardly call them facts."

The Group ignored the comment and continued, "It's well known that Group marsoliie are healthier, live longer and reproduce more often. We have the benefit of enhanced intelligence through the amalgamation of minds and shared histories and experiences, and we use up fewer resources because we're more efficient. Communal living is good for everyone, and it's the natural way. This is how our species evolved to be. Remaining Single at maturity is a deviation. It's bad for you. We just want to help you understand that."

The Group expanded its argument, and Carrie's attention wandered. It was only repeating what Errruorerrrrrhch had already told her, just in a longer, more roundabout and boring way. Her gaze drifted down. Below were the square shapes that she supposed were marsoliie residences. On the same level as her, but on the far side of the marsoliie, was a silvery shape. With a jolt she realised the object wasn't an animal or other natural inhabitant of Gaginion, it was an underwater scooter similar to her own.

Her head swivelling, she tried to find the

scooter's owner, but there didn't seem to be any non-locals there except herself. A different voice begin to speak, and her attention was drawn back to the meeting. It was the Single who seemed to represent the others. "On behalf of my fellow citizens I thank you for stating your views so concisely and eloquently." This brought a shuddering among the Groups that Carrie's translator conveyed as applause. "I'm happy to reassure you that I can be equally concise, if not more so.

"Our response is, even if we were to concede that everything you say is true—which we do not, though I agree there is research that seems to back up a little of what you say—even if we were to concede those points, it doesn't change the fact that we have the right to choose what we do with our own bodies. It's an inviolable right under Transgalactic Law, and adding Singles to your Groups without their consent is illegal, plain and simple."

"Ah yes, I'm familiar with this argument," replied the Group, "but it only applies if you consider your bodies to be your own, which under marsoliie natural law, the law of our species, they are not."

"Hey, get off me," came a third voice. On the edge of the gathering a Group had approached a Single and was holding onto one of its legs. The Single was tugging to get away.

"Stop that over there," called Carrie, performing a combination of star jumps and sit ups. Her arms and legs finally came to rest, and she saw movement near the two tussling marsoliie. It was the owner of the other water scooter. Invisible before due to his camouflage uniform, which was the colour of the sea, a Unity soldier was now visible against the background of the large Group. He was approaching the creature, a long staff with rounded tips in his hand. Carrie blinked and squinted. She'd been mistaken. The soldier wasn't a man, it was a large woman.

The soldier jabbed the Group in the middle with his staff, but it didn't relinquish its hold on the Single, who was beginning to turn limp. The Group pulled at the Single's leg, and it allowed itself to be dragged closer. The soldier jabbed the Group again, harder.

"This is outrageous," exclaimed the Single representative. "This is exactly the kind of thing we're talking about. Command your colleague to withdraw at once."

The attacking Group grabbed the staff, pulling the soldier towards it. She delivered a well-aimed kick, which broke the Group's grasp. But another leg came up and quickly grasped the soldier around her middle.

"Hey," shouted Carrie, and backflipped. As soon as she righted herself, she tugged on her tether, pulling her water scooter over. Clamping her lips shut to avoid the temptation to say anything else, she leapt onto her vehicle.

"Please don't do that," called the Group to its fellow, "I know you're only trying to do the right thing, but now is not the time nor the place."

Carrie was already on her way over to help the soldier. The Group had released the Single, which was moving lazily, as if coming to its senses. The Group continued to battle with the soldier, however. Its tentacles were wrapped round her leg, arm and hips, but the soldier was putting up a good fight. She managed to free her staff from the Group's grip and drive it into its centre with a force that made Carrie wince. There was a roar, and the Group let go of the soldier's arm and leg. Then the tentacle holding the soldier's hips reeled in, drawing the soldier closer like a yoyo. She curled into a ball and turned head over heels, twisting the tentacle in a way that must have been very painful, for the Group finally let go. The soldier kneed the creature's middle and shoved it away from her with the sole of her foot. It pulsated once, then swam off slowly.

"I apologise for that," said the Group representative. Singles and Groups began chattering about the incident, and the meeting grew loud.

Impressed by the soldier's fighting skills but not wanting to risk having her words turned into physical contortions, Carrie gave her a thumbs up.

CHAPTER THIRTEEN – BLAST FROM THE PAST

By the end of the meeting, demarcation lines had been drawn up and agreed by the Group and Single marsoliie, with many expressions of sadness on the part of the Groups, who complained about the Singles' determination to 'divide the community'. Satisfied she had done a reasonable job—performing several strange and occasionally painful gyrations—and the discussion had positive outcome, Carrie headed back to the Council starship.

She hadn't gone far before her respirator indicator needle reached the centre of the dial. She stopped her water scooter to insert a new tablet. The machine floated idly round as she was fiddling with the receptacle in her helmet. After pulling out the old tablet and slotting the new one in place, she glanced up. Behind her was the silver vehicle of the Unity soldier, who was following in her wake. She waited to allow the soldier time to catch up, wondering what she was doing. Was the Unity starship in the same vicinity as the Council's? The woman reached Carrie, but she didn't stop. She sped past without even a glance in Carrie's direction.

Carrie shrugged and started up her vehicle. Her coordinates led her along the same route at the soldier. The Council starship emerged from the gloom ahead. The soldier was heading straight for it. Frowning, Carrie tried to remember if she had seen any Unity presence on board. She was sure she hadn't. Maybe the soldier was lost? But if that was the case, why didn't she stop and ask Carrie for help?

Curiosity gripping her, she turned her water scooter up to full speed, and sped off after the soldier. By the time she caught up, they were both at the ship. Hoping that as there were no marsoliie nearby her words wouldn't be converted to body language, she called out, "Hi, I'm Carrie." The soldier didn't reply, so she added, "Thanks for your help back there."

They were outside the airlock, and the soldier must have radioed her arrival because it was opening. Together, they swam in. The outer door closed, and the water began to drain out. Still the soldier said nothing. Carrie surreptitiously studied her form and enigmatic, opaque visor. The woman seemed familiar. Had she been on the squashpump planet during the hostage siege? Then realisation dawned. As the woman pulled off her helmet and her tawny gold hair tumbled about her shoulders, Carrie exclaimed, "Belinda."

***

"I don't BELIEVE that woman." Carrie threw her wet toolbox into the shower room, where it landed with a crash.

Eyeing the bag, which was dripping seawater, Dave asked "Who?" before returning to arranging his Council Officer's devices on the top of his locker.

"Belinda!"

"Belinda?" Dave stopped what he was doing and turned to face her. "Not...?"

"Yes, that Belinda," Carrie said, her eyes ablaze. "Half-dandrobian Belinda who Gavin brought in to take over from me. The Belinda who wouldn't let us get on board the paperclip with her to go the placktoid ship. The Belinda who refused to listen to the poor oootoon. THAT Belinda." She sat down with a thump on Dave's bunk.

"Don't sit there, you're all wet."

Carrie had forgotten she was still in her wetsuit. "Ugh, sorry. I'll have a shower." She grabbed a towel and went in, closing the door. "Hey, it's really clean in here," she called. While showering, she continued to talk loudly, telling Dave that Belinda was a Unity soldier now, and about her fight with the Group marsoliie, and how she came back to the Council starship and completely ignored Carrie while they were in the airlock, marching off as soon as the inner door was open. She came out of the shower room, rubbing her hair.

"Well, it certainly sounds like she hasn't changed much," said Dave.

"You can say that again," Carrie replied, dropping the towel on the floor. "But why's she here if she's a Unity soldier now? This is a Council ship."

"Maybe she had to deliver a message?" Dave pulled the weapon he had stolen out from under his bunk. He lay down and began to examine it.

"Hey, haven't you got rid of that yet?" asked Carrie.

"I haven't had a chance." He held the green object up to the light. "What a feat of design, though, don't you think? So much power packed into such a small package. I wonder how it works?" He brought it closer to his eyes and peered at it.

"Don't go trying to open it up, for goodness sake," said Carrie. "You could release deadly radiation, or blow up the ship." She brushed her hair. "Honestly, Dave, you have to get rid of it, and quickly."

"No time now. We have to go for a meeting."

"Really? I thought we were finished for the day."

"Yes, really. It's in the itinerary. It's a plenary session to go over our experiences during the practical training."

Carrie stopped brushing and sighed. "A plenary session, like where everyone gets together and talks? I hate those."

Dave rolled his eyes. "Come on, it's going to start in five minutes."

Flattening the stubborn kink in her hair with her hands, Carrie said, "Okay, I'm ready."

"Aren't you going to put your stuff away?"

"What stuff?"

Dave picked up the towel and Carrie's pyjamas from the floor and pushed them into her hands.

"Oh, *that* stuff," she said, smiling sheepishly.

As they left their cabin, Gavin appeared round a corner in the corridor. His children seemed to have swollen since Carrie had last seen them. She speculated that they must be approaching their first moult. Gavin was moving more slowly than usual, possibly finally feeling their weight. "Carrie, I would like to have a little chat with you."

"Sorry, Gavin," said Dave, grabbing Carrie's arm and pulling her along. "No time. We're late for a meeting." He shuddered as they left the insectoid alien behind. "I hope we go home before those things grow up and leave Daddy."

They were the last to arrive at the plenary session. It had already begun, and the trainees were taking turns to talk about what they had learned during the mediation process. The faceless hairy alien, who didn't seem to have a name, was explaining how he had successfully guided the marsoliie to split into small teams of several Singles and one Group, and discuss their feelings. Next it was the turn of the squashpump. She had encouraged the marsoliie to brainstorm words they associated with the current conflict. As the squashpump spoke, Carrie felt a yawn rising in the back of her throat. Why did people have to go into so much detail about everything?

Dave nudged her. Carrie's attention returned to the meeting. There was an expectant silence. It was her turn to speak. "Oh, erm, well, my Groups and Singles came to an agreement to, to divide up the territory and stay out of each other's way, until they—"

"That is a satisfactory interim outcome," interrupted Errruorerrrrrhch, "but can you explain what you *did* to facilitate this productive discussion the marsoliie apparently had?"

Carrie blinked. She tried to remember what she had said. "Erm, well, I'm not sure I did anything in particular. It just seemed to happen." There were some titters. Her face grew hot. "I made sure they listened to each other, mostly." She waited for the inevitable cutting remark from Errruorerrrrrhch. But what else could she have said? It was true. She had done very little talking. The Singles and Groups had come to the agreement by themselves. All she had done, after the Group's fight with the Single and Belinda, was to interfere as little as possible as long as the two sides were prepared to listen.

But Errruorerrrrrhch wasn't paying attention to her anyway. The manager's head had swivelled from horizontal to vertical, which meant she was communicating with someone or something far off. Her head resumed its normal position, and she spoke. "It seems we have a new recruit to the training programme. She is approaching at this moment so I will take this opportunity to introduce you." The door at the back of the room opened, and the trainees turned to see who would enter. " I would like you to welcome..." A figure appeared. Carrie's spine stiffened. The new trainee had exchanged her black and silver Unity uniform for the fluorescent orange of the Council. She paused, presumably for effect, in the doorway, statuesque and beautiful. "...Belinda."

CHAPTER FOURTEEN – TOO CLOSE FOR COMFORT

Carrie, Dave, Audrey and the oootoon sat at one table at dinner, Belinda, the hairy thing, the squashpump and the insectoid alien sat at another. The light was by itself in the corner, flashing intermittently. Recharging? Carrie wondered. Belinda had her table in stitches with stories she was telling, and from the glances Carrie received from that direction, it seemed most of the stories were about her.

"I bet she's telling them about my first assignment," she said to Dave.

He shrugged. "What if she is? You uncovered the truth about what the placktoids were doing and revealed they had developed or stolen gateway technology. You did a great job, in the end."

Carrie frowned at the final three words of her friend's comment. "Yes, I did discover all of that. Not that anyone at the Council seems to appreciate it. Or else I wouldn't be here."

Dave became very interested in his meal, which was strange because it tasted like something that had already been eaten.

"So, you didn't get time to talk about what you did today, Dave," said Carrie, "what with Belinda hogging the end of the session telling everyone about her transfer."

"Are you talking about that new recruit?" asked Audrey. "Didn't she say she's half-dandrobian? I thought it was very interesting that she worked as a Liaison Officer before she decided on a career change and became a Unity soldier. Then she came back to the Council because resolving disputes peacefully is her true vocation. So cool."

Oh yes, very cool, thought Carrie. She wondered whether Belinda's poor performance on her assignment with the oootoon and placktoids had contributed to her 'career change' idea.

"We know all that," said the box of oootoon. "We were there at the plenary session, too, you know. Where were we? No, I don't remember that. Who are we talking about? The new one. Pay attention."

Carrie sometimes wished she could fix her translator to screen out the oootoon. Listening to it explain how it had mediated for the marsoliie had been a farce. It couldn't agree with itself over what had actually happened. It was wonderful that the creature(s) had decided to separate itself from the rest of...itself...back on its planet, to help the Council deal with the placktoids, but she couldn't see how it could help, practically.

"SO," she said, steepling her fingers, "what did you do today, Dave?"

Her friend put down his fork, gratefully, it

seemed. "Well, you know, I just reasoned with them. Got them to explain their perspective, then to try to see things from the other side's point of view. They talked about what had happened in the past. The Singles said how they had lost their friends to Groups, and the Groups explained how they felt they'd enriched the life of every Single who joined them." He shook his head slightly. "I can't say they came to any firm resolutions by the end of the meeting, but I think it calmed tensions a lot."

Carrie sighed. "That sounds really good." She rested her chin in the palm of her hand. "I wish I'd thought of that." But of course Dave was better than her at being a Liaison Officer. Hadn't his brain scan found he was ninety-seven per cent compatible with the job, while her result was only thirty-four?

Something ran over Carrie's foot, and she jumped. She peered under the table and blanched at the sight of one of Gavin's children climbing her trouser leg. Turning, she saw her Manager had entered the canteen. His offspring were scattering from him as he came, climbing onto tables and chairs and up the walls.

"Right, well, I'm stuffed," said Dave, pushing his nearly full plate away. "See you later." He stood, then froze rigid. His eyes sought Carrie's in a wild, desperate stare as his face turned white. She gave a small scream and pointed. A baby insectoid alien was scaling his shoulder, its little antennae waving.

"Oh, that is adorable," said Gavin as he

approached. "She does not usually climb on other people. She must like you."

Sweat beaded on Dave's forehead. His eyes pleaded with Carrie. She gently removed the bug that was crawling up her trousers and placed it on the floor before reaching for the one on her friend. "I'll see if I can—"

"No, no," said Gavin, "please do not remove them yourselves. It is important that they learn to do as they are told."

"Right," said Dave through his teeth.

An aroma of roast beef mixed with aniseed filled the air as Gavin spoke to the errant child in his species' language. Carrie's translator conveyed the words to her mind. "Now then, Jessica, I am certain the nice gentleman would prefer it if you did not climb on him. Is that not so?" The final remark was in English and addressed at Dave, who gave a stiff nod. "So you must climb down immediately."

But instead of climbing down, the insect scrambled higher, up Dave's neck and onto his head. Carrie wondered if he would actually faint. She prepared to catch him.

"Jessica. Did you hear me?" Gavin's child sat in Dave's hair, where it seemed to be practising moving its inner jaws in and out, catching a few strands each time. Dave trembled. "I do apologise. She is about to moult, and at this stage they can be rather difficult to control."

"I see," squeaked Dave.

"I am afraid it is necessary that I use a threat.

Most regrettable, but I can see no alternative. I am a first-time father, you see, and unaccustomed to—"

"Go right ahead." Dave's tone was strangled.

"Jessica, if you do not descend from the nice gentleman immediately I will be forced to...to take you to see your mother." Almost too fast to be seen, the young alien scampered down Dave, across the floor and out of the room. Like a building demolished with explosives, Dave collapsed to his chair, but he quickly recovered and grabbed his bag as if to leave. Turning, he stopped and staggered. The canteen was being overrun with Gavin's children. They were playing tag, eating leftovers and swinging from the backs of chairs. Dave clutched his bag to his chest and he slowly resumed his seat, his eyes darting to and fro all the while, as if searching for an escape route.

"I am pleased that we finally have time for a private chat, Carrie," said Gavin. Audrey and the oootoon took the hint and left the table.

"Oh, yes, I remember, did you want to tell me something?"

"I was hoping to inform you about your colleague, Belinda, before you encountered her. I was aware you would both be present at the marsoliie meeting. Your initial encounter on the oootoon planet was quite unfortunate, and I was hoping to smooth the path towards a reconciliation between the two of you. After all, your Liaison Officer roles involve improving relations and resolving differences amicably. It would be regrettable if we were unable to set a good example in this area within our own ranks, do you not think so?"

Gavin's words hit home, and Carrie bit her lip. He was right. She should be trying to be friends, not holding onto a grudge against Belinda, no matter how hard the half-dandrobian made it for her. She really wasn't a very good Liaison Officer. "Yes, you're right, I suppose. But why was she working as a Unity soldier? And what's she doing here?" Gavin would know the truth, and he wouldn't put a gloss on it.

"Hmm...well, it is not appropriate for me to tell you the personal details of another member of staff, but her performance during your first assignment was not satisfactory, and she appeared unable to take responsibility for her behaviour. She resigned in order to try soldiering with the Unity. That role was apparently not a good fit for her either, and she requested a transfer back to the Council. As we are currently running a recruitment drive, and it looks as though one of the candidates here will not pass the programme, we felt it was an opportune moment to accept her application. By attending the remedial training her former faults will be addressed and hopefully Belinda can rejoin the Council."

Gavin continued to talk about how Belinda could catch up on the courses she'd missed, but Carrie didn't hear him. All she could hear was his voice echoing in her head: *one of the candidates here will not pass the training.* Did he mean her? He must mean her. But if he meant her, why would he just come right out and say it like that? *He means someone else*, she decided, *or he wouldn't tell me*. Then another thought struck her—this must be Gavin's way of warning her that she was going to fail if she didn't improve. Her heart sank. Another of her Manager's children began climbing her leg, but she didn't notice.

She was already trying her best. How was she supposed to do better?

CHAPTER FIFTEEN – A WET MESS

Overnight, the Transgalactic Council starship moved to a new location on Gaginion. Lying in her bunk, Carrie felt the ship's motion through the water. It rose and fell gently, but the soothing movement didn't help her sleep. Over the course of the week, her anger about being made to do remedial training had been replaced by anxiety that the decision had been correct, that she was actually useless at her job. And now her fear was heightened by Belinda's presence. It would be bad enough to fail, but it would be soul-destroying if Belinda passed but she didn't.

She turned onto her side and listened to the sound of Dave's breathing in the bunk below, reminding her of the weapon he had stolen and still hadn't got rid of. Her focus of worry shifted. Dave was a much better Liaison Officer than her, his stealing habit aside. He deserved to do the job, and it seemed as though he was getting over his wariness and enjoying himself. But if he was found with that weapon he'd be kicked off the course at the very least. That would be wrong. He could be a real asset to the Council.

Eventually, she began to drift off and her thoughts became dream-like. As an image of Dave, Belinda and herself standing in a triangle, throwing the weapon to each other like a bomb about to explode, swam hazily through her mind, she fell asleep.

Due to her bad night, Carrie overslept again the next morning. After waking her twice, Dave had to shake her to make her get up and get ready. They were continuing with their practical training that day. The ship had moved to an area of the planet that had a dense population of marsoliie, and Errruorerrrrrhch explained at the airlock that relations between the Singles and Groups in this region were particularly strained. If the Council mediation attempt wasn't successful, civil war was likely to break out.

"Ordinarily, we would not assign such a sensitive mediation process to trainees, but there are insufficient experienced staff available to address this problem. You have not been able to follow galactic news while aboard ship, but I can tell you that the Council and Unity continue to comb the galaxy for the placktoids without success. It is feared that, wherever they are, the placktoids are approaching a major move to assume complete control of galactic resources and affairs.

"But, to return to your assignments for the day, due to the more strained relations, where a Unity soldier is not available to assist we have selected two trainees to work together. You will be in radio contact. Please consult your briefing devices for more detailed information. Now, are there any questions?"

Carrie eagerly pulled out her transparent

tablet. It would make sense to pair her with Dave. They knew each other and shared a room. She scanned the screen. Yes! She did have a partner, and it was—

"Hurry up," said Belinda. "I want to get this over with as soon as possible." The half-dandrobian shoved a helmet at her.

Carrie's face fell. Of all the trainees they could have picked, it had to be her. She put the device back in her bag and snatched the helmet out of Belinda's hands. Then she remembered Gavin's words about getting along with her colleagues. That was easy enough when you were working with reasonable people, but Belinda took the biscuit in rudeness, arrogance and downright pigheadedness.

Outside the starship, Carrie slowly kicked her way over to the water scooters. Belinda swam past her and had hopped aboard a water scooter and zoomed away while Carrie was still fixing her briefing tablet in her dashboard. *Damn that woman. Can't she wait five minutes?*

The coordinates flashed, and Carrie set off. The water in this part of the planet was murkier than the previous place they had worked. She squinted as she peered through the gloom. Belinda was already quite far ahead, her vehicle glinting in the green light from above. Carrie increased her speed to try to catch up to her, but Belinda was going at full throttle, and she couldn't close the gap. The two travelled along for some time before there was a flash of brilliant light to Carrie's left.

Turning her head for a closer look, she caught her breath. Not far distant from her was a collection of small water creatures. In the glow fading from the flash, she could see them moving into a new, intricately detailed pattern. A second brilliant flash came, and Carrie shielded her eyes. What the animals were doing, she didn't know. Maybe it was courtship or mating behaviour, or maybe they were communicating with far distant members of their species, or maybe even her. Whatever the behaviour was for, it was beautiful and fascinating to watch.

Carrie gazed at the creatures' display for a short while before reluctantly drawing her eyes away. She had to get to the marsoliie meeting. If it were not for that, she could have stayed and watched them all day. Searching ahead, she could see no sign whatsoever of Belinda now. She started up her vehicle and sped onward. Her distance counter indicated she was already quite near. She should be able to see the marsoliie somewhere ahead, but there was no sign of them. Deciding it must be due to the murky water, she pressed on. But after another few moments' travel, when her distance counter stood at zero, she still saw nothing but empty ocean.

Stopping her waterscooter, she peered at her coordinates. She was sure the numbers were different from those displayed when she set off. As she watched, the numbers flickered and changed. She was right. They were different. But what did the fact they were changing mean? Was the marsoliie meeting moving?

Carrie hesitated. The obvious thing to do would be to contact Belinda by radio and ask her what was happening. But the thought of admitting she was lost left a bad taste in her mouth. She started up her scooter again and set off, following the new coordinates. Soon after, the coordinates changed again. Carrie hoped the new position was closer to her, or that at least that the marsoliie weren't moving so quickly she would never catch them up.

"Where are you?" Belinda's voice burst in her ear. "I've been waiting for you to arrive to begin the meeting. The marsoliie are very tense."

"I'm on my way, but..." The coordinates changed yet again.

"But what? Hey, keep back." Belinda's exclamation was accompanied by a rushing sound as, Carrie presumed, Belinda's translator converted her words to body language.

"Are you moving?" Carrie asked. "I keep seeing new coordinates."

"Moving? No, we've been in the same—stop that immediately. On behalf of the Transgalactic Council, I demand..." The rest of Belinda's words were lost in a swishes and bubbles.

Carrie gripped the handles on her water scooter. If the marsoliie weren't moving, why was she constantly seeing new numbers?

"Damn it, Carrie, get over here. The Groups are taking over the Singles. I can't control them by myself."

"I'm trying, but there's something wrong with

my briefing device. It keeps changing the coordinates."

"Arghh...keep away. Turn it off and on again you idiot. I'm recording this, you know."

Carrie hoped the final comment was directed at the marsoliie and not her. Belinda's advice about her briefing device was sound. Why hadn't she thought of it before? After quickly thumbing the plastic tablet off and on, the coordinates seemed to finally stabilise. She set off at full speed. But how many Singles had been taken by Groups while she'd been lost?

In front of her was a reddish patch of ocean that was growing larger. She let out a sigh of relief. This had to be the meeting place. As she drew close, however, her hands clenched to fists on her scooter handlebars. All she could see was Groups, everywhere. She scanned again for Singles, but she couldn't see any at all. Belinda was waiting for her among them, her hands on her hips.

"Don't tell me..." Carrie said as reached her colleague.

"I did my best, but you weren't here to help."

"Hey, it wasn't my fault my briefing device wasn't working properly."

"You took your time figuring it out. Why didn't you contact me sooner?"

"Because I...I..." Carrie couldn't see Belinda's face very well, but she was sure she heard a sneer in her tone. "You said you were recording them. Maybe the Council can use the evidence to make them give up the Singles they took?"

"It was an empty threat, and they knew it. The marsoliie are indistinguishable, and the Singles will already have lost all memory of what happened." She climbed aboard her water scooter. Her head facing forward, away from Carrie, she said, "I knew you were incompetent from the moment I saw you out of uniform on Oootoon. The success you had on that mission was pure luck, and you managed to tarnish my perfect record along the way. I predicted it wouldn't be long until you messed up, and I was right." She sped away, parting a collection of pulsating Group marsoliie as she went.

At first, Carrie seethed at Belinda's words, but as she returned to the Council starship her anger faded and her heart grew heavy.

CHAPTER SIXTEEN – ABOUT FACE

Carrie didn't dare hope Belinda would spare her when it came to feeding back to Errruorerrrrrhch and the other trainees about their encounter with the marsoliie, and she was right. The half-dandrobian went into excruciating detail as she related how she had been forced to single-handedly try to prevent the Groups from attacking the Singles, all the while waiting and waiting for her colleague to appear and lend a hand. She explained how, when Carrie had finally made contact, she'd had to advise her on the simple and obvious solution to equipment malfunction. She described how Carrie had appeared on the scene long after it was too late to save the Singles. She concluded with the fact that, as the Singles were in the last stages of losing their minds to the Groups who had captured them, they cursed the Transgalactic Council for allowing their entrapment.

Belinda didn't embellish her story with additional details. She didn't need to. Carrie's impulsive decision to forge ahead and not think carefully about what she was doing was apparent to every listener, none more so than herself. By the time Belinda stopped speaking, every eye on was on Carrie. She hung her head low, wilting under their gaze. Gavin had been right. The trainee who was going to fail was her. There was no doubt in her mind now.

"And what did you learn from your experiences today, Officer Hatchett?" Errruorerrrrrhch asked.

Carrie looked up. The other trainees waited patiently for her to speak. But she had nothing to say. There was nothing she *could* say that would justify her behaviour, nor return the captured Singles to their former status. She didn't know why she had even come to the session. It was all over for her. She lifted her bag to her shoulder, stood up and walked out.

***

"Carrie, I know you're awake," said Dave.

She opened her eyes to see her friend's concerned face level with her own as she lay in the top bunk. Hoping the marks of her tears weren't showing, she smiled bravely. "I was tired. I thought I'd have a lie down. How did the rest of the session go? What was your day like?"

Dave rested his elbows on her bed. "It was okay. A bit boring, really. No one made much headway. The Groups around here are much too vicious. They won't listen to reason. Are you okay? I was worried about you after you left the room without giving your feedback."

Carrie sat up on her elbows. "Yes, I'm all right. It was just listening to Belinda going on like that, and everyone hearing how I messed up,

I couldn't stand it. What happened to those poor Singles was all my fault."

Dave's eyebrows lifted. "All your fault? I don't think anyone thought that. We all had a hard time today. Even with both of you there, you probably couldn't have stopped what happened."

"I could have tried at least." Tears pricked her eyes again. "I don't know. Maybe if it hadn't been Belinda of all people, telling everyone what I'd done."

"Hmm, yeah, she didn't pull any punches, did she? But you showed her up when you were on your very first job. Put her to shame. If she had taken over from you, like Gavin planned, no one would have found out what the placktoids were doing. She needs to get her revenge to feel better about herself."

Carrie frowned. She hadn't thought of it like that, but maybe Dave had a point.

"Are you getting up?" he asked. "It's nearly time for dinner."

"No, I'm going to give it a miss. I'm not feeling up to facing them all yet, and I really am tired. It's been a long week."

"Well, if you're sure. I heard the chef's pulling out all the stops tonight. It's bound to taste fantastic."

Laughing, Carrie said, "He can't top the mouldy carrots and sludge flavour of last night's dinner."

Her friend nodded. "You're right. And to think I've been missing out on sludge-flavoured food all these years." The doorbell sounded, and Carrie and Dave looked at each other quizzically. Had Gavin come back for another visit, his dreadful children in tow?

"You open it," said Dave. He went into the shower room.

Carrie jumped down from the bunk and opened the door. She took a step back. It was Belinda. The gorgeous, statuesque, tawny-haired woman stood in the corridor with her hands on her hips and her lips pressed together in a slight grimace. "Aren't you going to invite me in, then?"

Stepping aside, Carrie mind whirred as to why the half-dandrobian was there. Had she come to gloat some more? Dave appeared. "Hi, Belinda."

"Hello. It's Dave, if I remember rightly?" He nodded. "Do you mind if I sit down?"

"Sure," said Dave, "but there's only..." He indicated the lower bunk. Belinda lowered her well-shaped bottom to the bed. An awkward pause stretched out, during which Carrie and Dave exchanged glances.

"I'm sorry," said Belinda, flushing and looking down. "I'm not used to doing this."

"Look," said Carrie, heatedly, "if you want an apology or something..." Dave placed a hand on her arm.

"No, that isn't it." Belinda looked up into Carrie's eyes. "In fact..." she let out a heavy breath, "in fact...I'm the one who should apologise."

"You should...what?" Carrie's eyes grew wide.

Belinda sighed again, and her shoulders lifted and fell. "I've been a bit of an arse, haven't I?" Carrie was about to answer, then realised the question was rhetorical. "I think I need to explain some things," Belinda continued. "You see, I used to be one of the top Liaison Officers. That's why Gavin called me in to take over from you on Oootoon. After five years' service, my record was spotless. I suppose I'd become too confident, and complacent. I thought I was the bee's knees, to be honest." She paused, and broke eye contact with Carrie. "Frankly, you made me look like a fool." She gave a little shake of her head. "But, well, I deserved it. You were right and I was wrong. Though that was very hard for me to accept at the time. In fact, I didn't accept it. And from then until now, I've been telling myself that it was all just a fluke.

"After what happened today, I thought, that confirms it. I couldn't wait to get back here and tell everyone what an idiot you were. And I did..." she smiled wryly, "...with great relish, enjoying every word. But I expected you to try to defend yourself. *Go on, bluster yourself out of that*, I thought to myself. I was surprised when you didn't. You knew you'd messed up, and you didn't try to justify it. You just walked out. And instead of feeling vindicated, I just felt sort of hollow.

"You see, when I was in your position, I couldn't admit it to myself. But you did. You were better than me, again. So..." She stood and held out her hand. "Let's put an end to this silly feud between us, and let bygones be bygones, okay?"

Her mouth slightly agape, Carrie took the offered hand, and the two women shook. Without another word, Belinda left.

"Did that just happen?" Carrie asked as the door closed.

"Either that or we're both in the same dream."

Carrie sat down with a bump. "And that was Belinda, right?"

"It certainly looked like Belinda, but the words didn't seem to match the personality."

Carrie laughed, then stopped. "Oh, I get it."

"What?"

"We're forgetting she's half-dandrobian."

"You mean you think she's up to something?"

"Exactly. I wonder what it is?"

Dave shrugged. "Who knows? I'm going to dinner. It'll be over soon. Maybe I'll talk to Belinda and try to find out what her game is. If there's anything edible I'll bring you some back."

"Thanks."

After her friend left, Carrie went to take a shower. She marvelled at how clean Dave kept it, apparently effortlessly. She wondered if she should invite him to move in. He obviously loved cleaning, and she hated it, so they were the perfect match. He could bring his boyfriends over whenever he liked, she wouldn't mind. As she turned the shower off, she heard an announcement being broadcast. She wrapped a towel around herself and went out into the cabin to hear it better. It was Errruorerrrrrhch speaking.

"I repeat. A weapon is missing from the target practice room. It is presumed stolen. Remain exactly where you are while the ship is searched. Anyone moving from their current location will be immediately detained."

CHAPTER SEVENTEEN – THE GREAT ESCAPE

Carrie's knees turned to water. It must be the weapon Dave had taken. The weapon that was under his bed that very minute. She lifted the mattress. There it was. He still hadn't put it somewhere else like she'd told him to. She let out a gasp of frustration as she tried to figure out what to do. Spinning on her heel, she scanned the cabin. Was there somewhere she could hide it? The weapon was very small. Surely there must be somewhere they wouldn't think of looking?

But there didn't seem to be anywhere that wasn't an obvious hiding place. The beds, bags and lockers would be searched immediately. She felt behind the mirror-communication screen, but there were no gaps. It was fixed firmly to the wall. The shower room? Stepping inside, she searched the room with her eyes. Maybe she could put the weapon down the drain, or flush it down the toilet? She dropped it into the bowl, but it lay stubbornly at the bottom after flushing, and the drain in the shower was not removable. Everything else, the walls, ceiling and floor, were one piece of smooth ceramic.

Carrie's heart raced. How long did she have

before they came to search? And what was Dave doing, stuck in the canteen? What was he thinking? She hoped he hadn't confessed already, imagining the game was up. He didn't deserve to be punished for taking the weapon. They wouldn't understand he didn't intend any harm; that he would have returned it if he'd had the chance. She wrung her hands. She had to save her friend, she just had to.

Then the answer came. She slowly sat down on Dave's bunk. Of course. If they came to the cabin and found her with the weapon, they would assume she'd taken it. And she wouldn't correct them. She was going to fail the training anyway, so she might as well do something good and save Dave's skin. He was a better Officer than her. The brain scan had said so, and everything she'd done that week had proved it.

Now that she'd made the decision, she felt oddly calm, as if a weight had been lifted from her shoulders. All week she'd been stressing about passing the training. Now it was all over and out of her hands, she didn't have anything to worry about any more. Or did she? She gripped the weapon. She was assuming she would just be kicked off the course, but maybe there was a worse punishment in store for her. What happened to thieves under transgalactic law? Would she go to prison? Carrie swallowed. She remained determined to take the blame for the theft, but she wondered if there was some way to soften the blow about to fall, or someone who could help her? Someone who might help a friend?

A slow smile formed on her face. She would have disobey the order to stay where she was, but now that she was going to take the rap anyway, what did she have to lose?

***

Carrie steeled herself as the cabin door opened. She peeped inside, but, apart from one occupant, the room was empty.

"Carrie, what are you doing here?" asked Gavin. "You must return to your room at once. We cannot move about the ship. There has been a...ah. I see."

Carrie's palm was open, and in it rested the small green weapon. She stepped into the room and looked around. "Where are your children?"

"They are moulting at the moment. Carrie—"

"Where?"

"Where what?"

"Where are they moulting?" She wondered if a hundred larger versions of Gavin's offspring were about to pile out of the shower room. Except he didn't seem to have a shower room. Or a bed. All there was in the room apart from Gavin and a communication screen was a large hole in the floor.

"My children are in a room in a secluded area of the ship where they will not be disturbed. Carrie, I am most disappointed in you. I would never have believed you capable of stealing."

"There's a lot about me you don't know, Gavin. And one of those things is that I'm a thief.

An out and out criminal. Yes, I took this. I stole it."

"I—I do not know what to say. I am not sure why you have come to me to confess your guilt. It would perhaps have been better to wait in your cabin and not disobey the command."

"The thing is, Gavin, I think we can agree everything's over for me now. I'm going to wait here quietly until the search reaches this part of the ship. But I wanted to ask you what's going to happen, and is there anything I can say or do that might mean they'll deal less harshly with me?"

Her insectoid manager chittered. He crawled to and fro. He wiggled his antennae. His one hundred eyes blinked. "No, there is nothing at all. What is the English expression? You have come to the end of the road, I am afraid."

Voices, shouting, came from the corridor. It sounded like one of the Council's managers. "Stop, stop immediately. Return to your room at once."

Gavin went to the door and opened it. Beyond his bronze head, Carrie saw several of his children, larger now, scamper past. "Oh, the little rascals, they've escaped," Gavin exclaimed. A small insectoid alien ran into the room, and scuttled around its edges and out again. Its father made a swipe at it as it passed, but he missed. "This is most unfortunate. What am I to do? There will be absolute chaos." A Manager came running down the corridor, closely followed by the chef.

"Will you please control your children," shouted the manager.

"They are just a little high-spirited," called Gavin. "They will calm down soon enough. Please be gentle. They do not mean any harm." He turned to Carrie. "I must leave you. I must gather my children and discuss with them the inadvisability of running recklessly around the ship. Please wait here. I am sure the search will be resumed when my little ones are returned to their room." As he was leaving, he paused halfway through the door. "Not you as well. This is most irregular. Humans will never cease to amaze me. You should not be moving around the ship." He was talking to someone in the corridor, but Carrie couldn't see who it was. Then the person stuck his head around the door.

"I thought I might find you here," said Dave. "All hell's broken loose. Gavin's kids are all over the place. Everyone's left the canteen to try and catch them. Have you got it?"

Carrie nodded and opened her hand to show Dave the weapon. He grimaced.

"So you were aware she had stolen the weapon?" asked Gavin. "This crime is compounded. Dave, you are an accessory, I am sorry to say. Oh dear, this day is indeed going from bad to worse."

Dave raised his eyebrows. "She...? But I'm the one who—"

"Gavin, weren't you going to look for your children?" asked Carrie. "Look, there goes another one," she added, as a miniature Gavin darted past.

"Yes, you are correct. I must...but neither of you may leave this room, do you understand?" Two more of the manager's offspring scurried down the corridor.

"Yes," said Carrie, "we understand completely. But if by some strange chance we were to leave, in the confusion I mean, and put the weapon somewhere that was safe, but where it would be found, then...?"

The insectoid alien turned and re-entered the room, his antennae waggling wildly. "No, no, no. That would not be acceptable. I could never condone such behaviour. What you have done is utterly deplorable. I am sure you intended no harm, but stealing a weapon, especially one of such vital importance in the effort to control the placktoids, a top secret—"

"What weapon?" said Dave.

"The weapon Carrie stole, of course," said Gavin.

She held it out on the flat of her palm. "I can't see anything, can you, Dave?"

"Nope, nothing at all."

"Oh, really," exclaimed Gavin. "I know what you two are doing. It is no use...I—I must call someone to..." Another of his children appeared, climbing the corridor wall. "I must...I must go and find my children. Please remain here. This matter is not resolved."

As he left, Carrie high-fived her friend.

"Do you think he'll tell someone?" asked Dave.

Carrie smiled. "I think he'll probably *forget* in all the confusion." Lights began to flash, and an announcement sounded.

"Emergency. Emergency. All managers and senior staff report immediately to the central office."

CHAPTER EIGHTEEN – HOME TRUTHS

The missing weapon did indeed seem to be temporarily forgotten in the new crisis. The senior Council management held a private conference in their staff office, staying mum about what the emergency was, while Carrie and Dave, along with the other trainees, were given the task of catching Gavin and Errruorerrrrrhch's escaped children. The insectoid kids had quickly figured out the pheromone keys to every door on the ship, and they had spread everywhere. When the trainees found them, they were supposed to return them to their room, where they were to be kept locked in and guarded.

Carrie and Dave had been assigned to search the ship's engine room. Carrie was disappointed by the place. She had expected massive dilithium crystals and intense engineers with regional accents, but in fact the room contained only a large number of pipes, running at various angles across the walls and ceiling. "It's a bit underwhelming, isn't it? How do you think the engine works?" she asked Dave.

"If we knew that, humans wouldn't be stuck on Earth, would they?"

"Hmpf." Carrie put her hands on her hips as she surveyed the room. The pipes created nooks and crannies just big enough to hold a naughty immature insectoid alien, but they were very difficult for a human to see between and behind. They would have to feel around each pipe and in each crevice. The special dexterity and sensitivity of human hands was the reason the Managers had given for their selection for the job, but Carrie suspected Gavin had recommended them as a punishment for the weapon-stealing affair.

Dave peered into a shadowed corner. "I'll help find them, but I'm not touching the little monsters."

"Oh come on, they're kind of cute, don't you think?"

"You don't actually mean that, do you."

"No, you're right. I don't." Carrie squatted down and peered under a large white pipe that hummed. When she saw nothing underneath the pipe, she reached behind it, running her hand along the farther side. She tried to push aside thoughts of what the little escapees felt like. Hard, articulated and wriggly, she remembered from the encounter in the canteen. Did they bite? She shuddered, and noticed Dave had returned to the middle of the room and was looking about uncertainly. She straightened up. "I'll tell you what, I'll search this side. You search over there." She pointed. "Then we'll meet in the middle."

He sloped off to the opposite end of the room

and began casually inspecting it. Carrie sighed and resumed her search.

"I forgot to ask what you were doing back there, in Gavin's room," said Dave.

"Oh, that doesn't matter now. Forget about it. Damn." One of Gavin's children had shot out from a high corner. It dashed across the ceiling before disappearing into a dark recess. "Well we know there's at least one in here. I wonder if I can climb up there?"

"When I heard the announcement in the canteen, about the weapon," said Dave, "I panicked. I didn't know what to do. And of course, I couldn't do anything anyway. I couldn't leave, and I couldn't contact you."

"They were bound to find out eventually." Carrie stepped onto a pipe and grabbed the one above. "They must have taken stock of the equipment and noticed they were one weapon short."

"Yeah, you were right. I should've gotten rid of it a long time ago."

"You shouldn't have taken it in the first place, but never mind. What's done is done. It's over now. That was a good idea of yours to put it in Errruorerrrrrhch's office after we left Gavin's room. As soon as the Managers are out of their meeting she'll find it, and no one will be any the wiser as to who put it there."

"Yes, that's a weight off my mind. But you still didn't answer my question. Why did you go to see Gavin? What were you telling him? From what he said, he seemed to think *you'd* taken it, and you'd gone there to confess."

"Like I said, it doesn't matter now." Carrie stepped up onto another pipe and felt behind it.

"Is that what happened? Is that why you were there?"

Carrie didn't answer, unsure what to say. She continued to climb the pipes. A juvenile insectoid alien ran out from behind a pipe and over her hand. She gave a squeal and jumped down. The immature insect, going too fast, slipped off the pipe and fell to the floor next to Carrie. She threw herself over it. "I think I've got it. Chuck me the bag."

Dave tossed her the bag they'd been given for transporting the escapees. She caught it in one hand and felt beneath her with the other. "Got you," she exclaimed, and withdrew a struggling alien. After pushing it into the bag while it protested with a noxious stench, she pulled the tie closed and threw it back to Dave. "You hold onto this while I search the rest of the room."

Her friend caught the bag and quickly put it down. "Carrie, answer me, did you go to Gavin to tell him you were the thief? To take the rap for me?"

Exhaling heavily she answered, "Kind of, but it made sense, you know? I'm going to fail the course. Gavin as much as told me so, but you'll make a great Liaison Officer. I thought I might as well take the blame so the Council doesn't miss out on having you."

"What?" Dave took a step towards her. "That's insane. I mean, I appreciate it. That was an amazing thing for you to do. You're a great friend. But, you're good at your job. You aren't going to fail. Whereas me, well, I have no idea what I'm doing. I can barely swim even."

"Huh, there's a lot more than swimming involved. You've done really well, especially considering you only came along to do me a favour." She began climbing again, heading for the recess where the first insect they had seen was hiding. "I try. I want to help, I really do, but I can't seem to do anything right. Things just go to pot whenever I appear on the scene, and I don't know why. I've given up trying to figure it out."

"Well, firstly that isn't true. You've done great work—"

"No, I've just been lucky, as Belinda pointed out."

"—and secondly, if you just thought things through a bit more..."

"What do you mean, if I thought things through more? I think things through all the time. I don't know what you're talking about." She reached into the hole. "Hmm...it isn't there. It must have moved while we weren't looking." She began climbing down.

"I mean it, Carrie. Every time you do something stupid, I swear, it's just because you're being reckless and impulsive. If you just thought before you acted, you wouldn't have half the problems you do."

Carrie's mouth opened to an O as she reached the ground. "Reckless and impulsive, am I?" she exclaimed. "Thanks very much. After I take the blame for your kleptomania, this is the gratitude I get. Insults from someone who's supposed to be my friend." She snatched the bag out of Dave's hand.

"Carrie, I'm just trying to help."

"Well, I can do without your *help*." She turned her back on him. "I've had enough of this searching. We're going to be here all day at this rate." She squared her shoulders and addressed the room. "Okay, I can see you all. I know exactly where you are, so you might as well come out now." After a moment, three insectoid children crawled from their hiding places, somehow looking abashed. Carrie put the bag on the floor and opened its mouth. "Game's over. In you get."

Dave looked on, shaking his head in awe, as Gavin's offspring trooped obediently into the bag. "You see—"

"Hmpf. Got some more insults to throw at me?" asked Carrie, pulling the ties closed and throwing the bag over her shoulder, while an odious smell emanated from the protesting aliens inside.

Carrie marched from the engine room into the corridor, where she bumped into and rebounded from Audrey. Ignoring Dave, Carrie accompanied the green blob trainee as she rolled to return her captured children to confinement.

Audrey related how she had saved one of them from a nasty death by checking inside an oven as the chef was about to turn it on. "Have you heard the rumour?" she continued.

"I haven't heard anything," replied Carrie. "I've been stuck in the engine room taking gibes from my best friend." She threw a derisive glance over her shoulder.

"Oh...er..."

"Never mind. What's the news? Do you know what the emergency is?"

"Yes," exclaimed Audrey. "Everyone's saying they detected a transgalactic gateway opening on the other side of the planet. *This* planet. And they think it's the placktoids."

CHAPTER NINETEEN – THE FINAL STRAW

"As you are aware, we are in a state of emergency. I will explain the nature of that emergency and our intended actions going forward." Errruorerrrrrhch addressed the trainees, who had been gathered in the canteen.

"I believe you may already know that placktoids have appeared on this planet, approximately four hundred and twenty-two clicks southeast from here. Yes, they came through a transgalactic gateway. Why they chose this planet to reappear is as yet unknown. There have been no other gateways detected, nor sightings of placktoids elsewhere in the galaxy. From the numbers currently present on the planet, we can surmise the majority of them remain hidden elsewhere."

Carrie rested her chin in her hand, wishing Errruorerrrrrhch would get to the point. What were they going to *do*?

"According to long-range surveillance, the placktoids are on an ocean bed that is relatively close to the surface. They are constructing buildings, and a gigantic net of some kind, which floats above their settlement. We have as yet, to be frank, no idea what they are planning."

Carrie raised her hand.

"We have informed the central Council and the Unity of the little intelligence we have. We currently await their response. Some of you may know already that, while troops and weapons up to a certain size can travel by gateway, starships cannot. They must use FTL propulsion, and so—"

Carrie raised her hand higher, lifting slightly out of her seat.

"—And so," continued Errruorerrrrrhch, louder, "until Unity battleships arrive, for protection from the placktoids we have only the gunship that was supplied to subdue aggression among the marsoliie. The military capacity of the gunship is insufficient to justify a preemptive attack on the placktoids. Of course, we can assume they know we are here—"

Carrie stood and waved.

"Sit down," Dave said.

"I just want to ask a question," Carrie hissed.

"—yet they do not, for the moment, seem intent upon approaching." Errruorerrrrrhch swivelled to face Carrie. "YES?" The whole room jumped.

"Could you explain what we're going to do?"

"AS I was about to say, we are not going to DO anything for the moment."

Carrie slumped down in her seat.

"The placktoids seem to be able to open a gateway wherever they choose across the entire galaxy. Therefore, there is no purpose in leaving.

If we were to leave this very moment, they could open a gateway right where I am standing and there would be nothing we could do about it. At least while we are here, the Council has representatives on hand to keep watch on their activities while larger forces make their way to the location.

"As to whether we will open a dialogue with the placktoids, that has yet to be decided. We await further instructions on the matter. In the meantime, we will not be returning you to your home planets. Gateway travel is once more prohibited to allow the Council to track unauthorised usage. Your training will continue as normal, with the exception that no long distance journeys will be allowed. If the marsoliie request mediation services, they must approach within one click of the ship.

"That is all. You are dismissed."

Carrie's eyes widened. "That's it?" She turned to Dave. "We're just going to sit here and do nothing?"

"Sounds like it."

Pushing back her chair so that the legs screeched along the ground, Carrie stood up. "Unbelievable. What about the marsoliie and all the other creatures? Aren't they going to do anything to protect them? This is just like what happened with the squashpumps. They just don't care."

Dave also stood. "Honestly, Carrie."

"Honestly what?" She followed him as he left

the canteen.

He was two strides ahead of her. "Never mind."

"No, tell me."

Dave lengthened his stride, and Carrie had to increase her speed to keep up.

"What's the point?" asked Dave. "I'll only get accused of insulting you."

"Oh, I get it. I'm being *impulsive* and *reckless* just because I happen to care what happens to innocent civilians? Because I think they should be protected from evil aliens like the placktoids? Nobody's been as close to them as I have. Nobody else understands what the placktoids are like, what they're capable of."

They had reached their cabin. As they entered and the door closed behind them, Dave turned to face Carrie, his face rigid. "Nobody understands them like you? Have you considered who you're talking to? I was there too, remember?" He jabbed a finger at his chest. "I went through it all right beside you. I was nearly killed by the placktoid commander." He bent down, picked a towel off the floor and went into the shower room.

"Then you should know exactly what I'm talking about. We need to do something, and now."

Returning, Dave picked up Carrie's pyjamas and other discarded clothes before putting them on her bed. "No, we don't."

"Yes, we DO, before it's too late."

Dave grabbed his hair in both hands and let go. "This is exactly what I'm talking about, Carrie. You think you have a monopoly on compassion? Errruorerrrrhch explained very clearly why we have to wait. But you didn't listen. You just want to run off and do something, anything. Whatever hare-brained plan comes into your head. You never think about the consequences of your actions.

"And look at this." He spread his arm wide, indicating the messy cabin, with Council devices and bits of rubbish scattered around. "More evidence of your thoughtless, inconsiderate attitude. All week I've been cleaning up after you. All week. I've had enough." He opened his locker and pulled out his bag. As he was filling it with his things, he continued, "I knew if I said anything to you...if I tried to make you understand what you were doing wrong, you wouldn't listen. You'd get offended. And I was right. You go on about Belinda being rude and pig-headed? Well, maybe the next time you feel like moaning about her, go have a look in there first." He pointed at the mirror before stuffing the last of his possessions into his bag.

Carrie stood dumbfounded through this speech. As Dave opened the door she managed to ask, "But, where will you go?"

"I don't know. But wherever it is, it'll be better than living with you."

Carrie watched the closed door for a long moment.

When it was clear her friend wouldn't be

coming back, she took down the T-shirt he had draped over the cabin window to block out the view of the ocean. She carefully folded it and placed it on the locker top. She would have to remember to give it to him the next time she saw him, whenever that might be. Going to the window, she gazed deep into the murky water. Far off, lights blinked in brilliant, intricate patterns. It must have been the creatures she had seen on her way to the most recent marsoliie meeting, where she had been tardy, and the Groups had taken all the Singles. She recalled stopping to watch beautiful lights, making herself late, then delaying further because she had been too proud to tell anyone about her confusion and too stupid to figure out what the problem was.

The green ocean light dimmed as a dark mass floated nearer overhead. It was the creature Carrie had spoken to, who had told her it would soon deal with any placktoids that arrived. She wondered if it knew that the mechanical aliens had indeed appeared, and if it had any plans for dealing with them. As her eyes grew used to the darkness of the water, she could make out a patch of red, which moved and pulsated. Group marsoliie, it had to be, probably patrolling, looking for Singles to annex. She ached to get out there and do something to protect them.

She frowned. Was this what Dave was talking about? Was she really reckless and impulsive? She had never seen him so angry. But it felt so wrong not to act. To just sit by and wait. It made her feel useless. Abruptly, she turned from the window and sat on the locker top. On the floor around her lay the stuff Dave had complained about. It did look a bit messy, she had to admit.

The room seemed very quiet and empty without her friend there. She wondered where he had gone. Maybe another trainee had room in a cabin. The squashpump didn't take up much space, though she imagined its room was rather damp. A sob rose in her throat, but she fought it down. She refused to cry, though whether it was out of defiance or because she didn't want to pity herself for her own mistakes, she wasn't sure.

CHAPTER TWENTY – DANCE UP A STORM

Sitting with Audrey and the oootoon at breakfast the following day, Carrie smiled too brightly and laughed and talked too loudly. She kept glancing about, as if looking for someone, and hardly touched her breakfast. When her eyes chanced upon Dave entering the canteen, she looked quickly away before he could see her watching him. After she had allowed sufficient time for him to get his breakfast, she looked in his direction again. He wasn't heading to her table, of course, but when she saw who he was sitting with, her spine stiffened. Belinda.

Was he sharing a cabin with her now? It made sense. The cabins for humans were large enough for two, and Belinda was a latecomer to the training course, so she would have been allocated a room all to herself. Too late, Carrie realised the half-dandrobian had seen her watching. She jerked her head away. Had Belinda smirked at her? She wasn't sure, but her cheeks burned.

She stirred the substance in her bowl, which might have been porridge if it hadn't tasted the same as the smell of a wet dog. She had eaten nothing for dinner and she should have been hungry, but she wasn't. Even her persistent pot belly was showing signs of defeat.

Is something wrong? Who are you talking to? Carrie. Carrie? Who's that? I think she's looking peaky, wouldn't you say? Maybe the food doesn't agree with her. Is it the food? You can ask for something else, you know dear. Whatever it is, I hope it isn't catching. Oh don't be silly, we couldn't catch a disease from a human. Is there a medic on board? You should go and—

"I'm fine," said Carrie, pushing her chair back to stand. It screeched so loudly the whole canteen stopped talking and turned to see where the noise was coming from. "I'm just not very hungry. Do you know what we're doing today?"

"Individual exercises," said Audrey. "You can choose from the list, according to what you need most practice in. Transgalactic law, the art of diplomacy and some other things. I can't remember exactly."

The green blob's words brought Carrie some relief. At least she wouldn't have to face Dave and his new half-dandrobian friend in a group class. She said goodbye and left the table, but as she approached the door, Errruorerrrrrhch appeared, forcing her to step back. "Wait a moment, please," said the Manager as she passed.

The insectoid alien rapped a table with a claw for attention. When the room had quietened, she said, "In this difficult, dangerous time, I am pleased to report some good news. Outside of Council mediation, the marsoliie have reached a new level of understanding. The Groups have agreed a moratorium on their activities, for the duration of the crisis at least. As is customary within this species, the Groups and Singles must perform a ritual dance, and we are all invited.

"Due to the current threat from the placktoids, the dance will take place directly outside the ship. The morning's activities will be postponed in view of this unusual opportunity for you, as trainees, to observe a culture in concord, as opposed to conflict. It is important that you understand the value of your roles within the Council, and how rewarding successful mediation is."

When Errruorerrrrrhch's speech was over, Carrie continued to her room. She was happy for the marsoliie, but the news didn't lighten her mood. She wasn't cut out to be a Liaison Officer. She was going to fail the course, and the Group and Single dance would be her final sight of the species. The thought made her sad. Their movements were beautiful and mesmerising.

To kill time, she cleaned the shower room and put away her things neatly. When the cabin was clean and tidy, and she had nothing else to occupy her, she watched the ocean outside her window, where the marsoliie were gathering.

Finally, the announcement came that they were to gather at the airlocks. Carrie quickly put on her swimsuit and wetsuit and grabbed her Officer toolbox, checking she had respirator tablets and the rest of her equipment. In the corridor, she saw Dave. He tried to catch her eye, but she looked away. The memory of his words still echoed in her mind.

When she was outside the ship, the cool ocean water soon warmed against her skin. Swimming relaxed her a little, as it always did. The sight of the swelling ranks of marsoliie also lightened her heart. Their pulsating passage was graceful, complex and delicate as they travelled the currents.

Audrey arrived and bumped her. "Can you see it?"

She looked around. What did Audrey mean? All she could see was the creamy ceramic Council ship, the staff and trainees and the marsoliie. "What?"

"Over there."

This phrase seemed redundant to Carrie. Audrey was pretty much a sphere, with no appendages to point with, but she bobbed in one direction and back again. Carrie looked the way she indicated, but she could see nothing but ocean. Unless? She squinted and looked again. A patch of water didn't seem to quite match its surroundings, as if something were there that looked almost, but not quite, the same as the rest of the ocean. "The Unity gunship?" It was camouflaged in the same way as the military uniforms.

Audrey bobbed up and down in affirmation. "And the soldiers have come out to watch the display, too, I think. It's hard to tell, but there might be some just there." As she spoke, a soldier drifted in front of the Council ship and became briefly visible.

An idea sparked in Carrie's mind. Maybe she could do as Belinda had done, and become a soldier? But no, she couldn't risk it. If Dave was right about her faults, she definitely wasn't soldier material.

The marsoliie Groups and Singles were gathered into one large crowd, and no more seemed to be arriving. The Council airlocks opened, and the managers came out, each insectoid alien encased in an individual bubble of air. Audience and performers were ready. The Dance began.

***

Carrie knew she would never forget that performance. Without any apparent signal, the marsoliie lifted as one in a glorious scarlet fountain that then split apart like a stupendous firework, spraying across the ocean. Each segment the movement created turned in on itself before opening out in sequence, creating unique, oscillating crimson snowflakes, which flowed and coalesced again into one. As the Dance continued, Carrie began to feel dizzy. She realised she had stopped breathing. She inhaled, and gasped as the marsoliie began another movement, faster and more complex than anything she had seen up to that point. And just when Carrie thought the Dance could not become more stunningly beautiful, the marsoliie wreathed themselves in threads of silver that shimmered in the ocean shadows, catching the rippling beams from above.

Carrie couldn't remember when or why she began to move. It was an effect of watching the marsoliie performance for sure. One moment she was motionless, transfixed, floating in the water, and the next she was dancing, her limbs clumsily mimicking the exquisite motion of the aliens she was watching. She was transported to another world, where she was one with the marsoliie. A Group or a Single, it didn't matter. The only thing that mattered was participating in the magnificent Dance.

Something bumped her. It was Audrey. "What are you doing? Everyone's watching you."

Broken from her trance, Carrie finally saw the Council staff and trainees were no longer regarding the marsoliie, but had turned towards her. She quickly drew in her limbs and cringed. With a heart of lead, she heard Dave's words again. She was being impulsive. She had been carried away in the moment, not thinking about what she was doing.

A manager came swimming over, his ten pairs of legs working the water. "Please be more careful, Carrie." It was Gavin. "You must remember that what to humans is mere personal physical expression, carries meaning to the marsoliie. They are perhaps concentrating too much on their own dance to observe yours at the moment, but you could have accidentally communicated something that would cause great offence."

Carrie swallowed. "Yes, you're right, I'm sorry."

Another voice crackled in Carrie radio. It was unfamiliar, but authoritative, loud and urgent. "Get back. Placktoids approaching rapidly. Council staff, back to your ship." It was the Unity captain.

Through a break in the disintegrating marsoliie ranks, Carrie glimpsed the metallic forms of the placktoids closing in. Beams shot out in the darkness. The Unity troops were firing the new weapons, but the placktoids were hidden behind the fleeing marsoliie. The troops fired only intermittently as the mechanical aliens drew closer.

The Council ship airlocks were open, and the managers and trainees swam hastily towards them. Before any of them arrived at the ship, something dark shot out, and like a massive, black, many-fingered fist, and the Council staff shuddered. The dark object was a net. It exploded into the marsoliie, enclosing hundreds. As quickly as it had appeared, the net closed. The struggling marsoliie fought and surged within as they were forced closer and closer together. Tightening into a ball of scarlet crossed with black lines, the captured marsoliie were being drawn away into the murky depths.

CHAPTER TWENTY-ONE – PLACKTOID PROPOSAL

The Unity gunship had clearly been anticipating an attack. Those few soldiers Audrey and Carrie had spotted were just a ruse to encourage the placktoids to think they were being complacent or they were unaware of the mechanical aliens' presence. From behind the gunship, quickly blending with the ocean around them, Unity fighter ships rose, firing as they came.

Carrie's mouth fell open as the laser beams shot through the water. She had never seen a battle before. All her life she'd watched and enjoyed scifi TV shows and films, but what was happening in front of her was real. Too real.

"Into the ship, into the ship," called Errruorerrrrhch.

Swimming away from the fighting, Carrie couldn't resist looking over her shoulder as she followed the other trainees to the airlocks. The marsoliie that hadn't been caught in the net were scattering. Panicked, their movements were uncoordinated and clumsy. They couldn't move out of the way quickly enough, and as the placktoids returned fire, several were caught in their rays and burst into ragged scarlet explosions, a cruel mockery of their earlier

Dance.

Carrie wailed at the sight of the destroyed marsoliie. The Unity fighters zoomed up and around, in and out of the marsoliie, seemingly trying to avoid hitting the innocent civilians. Meanwhile the massive net of trapped Groups and Singles, hopelessly entangled in the thick black wires, withdrew into the distance.

The soldiers must have already returned to the Unity ship for it rose through the water, its fighter ships following it. As the vessels breached the surface, the cascade of current and bubbles knocked Carrie away from the airlocks. They were all open, but she didn't know for how long. The Council staff were crowding in. When they were full they would have to close them to allow the occupants to enter the ship. She kicked her fins powerfully against the downward drag, propelling herself closer.

The nearest airlock was closing. She would never make it before it shut, so she swam as quickly as she could to the next, scooting under its closing door just in time. The wait inside the lock, as the water drained out and air entered, was agonising. As soon as the inner door opened wide enough for her to pass through she was under it and out into the corridor, pulling off her helmet and stripping her wetsuit as she went.

Pushing back her wet hair from her face, she ran to the nearest porthole. The ocean was still filled with scattering marsoliie. Through and beyond them, the placktoids fled, the huge net of marsoliie bobbing above their heads. In the distance, the ocean parted as Unity ships plunged in from above. Unable to fire directly down without hitting the captured marsoliie, they aimed at the placktoids laterally.

The scene became smaller, and Carrie realised the Council ship had started up and was withdrawing from the battle site. She pushed her face against the porthole, straining to see what was happening. There was a flash of light from the placktoids, followed by a massive boom. She gasped as the light hit the solid form of the Unity gunship and poured over it, enveloping it.

Then the shock wave came. The remaining marsoliie were hit first. Shattered to confetti they flew apart. Carrie grasped her mouth as a sob rose in her throat. The wave hit the ship, and she was thrown from her feet. Her head hit the wall opposite. She was spreadeagled across it as the wave lifted the ship and turned it on its side.

Trainees, Managers and other staff throughout the corridor sprawled and staggered. As the ship tipped further, Carrie wondered whether the shock wave would turn it right over. But gradually the ship righted itself and she found her feet again. As soon as she was upright, she ran back to the porthole. The battle scene was farther distant. The marsoliie were red dots. The placktoids were glints. The Unity ships were not to be seen. Carrie hoped with all her heart that they hadn't suffered serious damage. Errruorerrrrhch had said the gunship didn't have the firepower to defeat the placktoids, and she had been right.

"Are you okay?"

Carrie turned to see Dave's anxious face. "Yes, I'm fine. And you?"

"Yes, not too bad. That was one hell of an experience."

"And Belinda? And everyone else?"

"It looks like everyone made it back safely."

"Thank goodness."

"Yeah."

There was a pause. Carrie had so much to say, but then again there were no words for how she felt. All her anger at Dave, her embarrassment, her hurt, all of it melted away as she realised she could have lost her best friend. "Dave, I'm—"

He held out his arms, and they hugged.

***

The trainees were left in limbo with vague orders to tidy up and be on full alert while the senior staff dealt with the crisis. According to the grapevine, they were in frantic communication with the Unity gunship and Council and Unity Central Offices. Carrie was relieved to learn the gunship had quickly withdrawn once it became clear there was nothing they could do to free the captured marsoliie. Consequently, there were no serious casualties among the Unity soldiers.

When everything had been put to rights and there was nothing left for the trainees to do, they gathered in the canteen, where they speculated about what would happen next. The general consensus was that they should just leave immediately. Carrie was against the idea. She wanted them to do something to help. The Council didn't have the combative abilities of the Unity, but it did possess the skills of mediation and negotiation, which were sometimes more effective than firepower, she argued.

She couldn't erase from her mind the image of the trapped marsoliie. Anxiety ran through her at the thought of them. She was compelled to do something, anything to free them. But she wondered if maybe it was only her impulsiveness talking. She was on remedial training, and she was going to fail even that. Maybe she should leave the action to people who knew better than her, and wait for orders.

"It's horrible, waiting, isn't it?" said Audrey.

"I can't bear it," said Carrie. "I wish they would give us something else to do."

"They'll tell us soon, I think. We'll be going home by gateway any minute, like the way they sent Errruorerrrrrhch and Gavin's kids away as soon as the placktoids were sighted."

"I hope not. I don't want to go home. I want to help."

An announcement echoed in the room. "Trainees, please return to your rooms. We are here for the duration. Please return to your cabins and await further orders."

"Oh no," said Audrey, "I was hoping this was the end of it for us."

The announcement continued, "Carrie Hatchett, go directly to the staff office."

Carrie tensed and looked at Audrey, her eyebrows raised. What had she done? Had Gavin told them about the weapon? It seemed a funny time to be disciplining her, but she supposed they had nothing else to do while they waited for the placktoid crisis to unfold. All eyes, heads and antennae on her, she left the canteen.

Five managers awaited her in the large room. Two of them were Errruorerrrrrhch and Gavin, but she found it difficult to tell the others apart.

"Thank you for coming." Gavin's tone was polite and kindly. "Would you like to sit down?"

She looked around. Carrie smiled as she was reminded of the first time she had met her insectoid manager. "There's nowhere to sit."

"Ah yes. Well, please prepare yourself. I have something important to tell you, and the information may be something of a shock."

This was it. They were going to tell her she'd failed the training. They'd picked a helluva time.

"This afternoon's events are most regrettable. We tried to insist the marsoliie did not perform their ritual dance, but they were not to be put off. As it was, the placktoids took the opportunity to gather a large number all at once, when they had clearly been planning to capture them individually over time—"

"Get to the point," said a manager.

"Very well, very well. Carrie, we have received a communication from the placktoid commander. He is offering a bargain. It seems they had a particular purpose in coming to

Gaginion. In return for the release of the captured marsoliie, the commander is asking for..." Gavin turned to the other Managers. "I really must register my protest once more. She should not be informed. This is far too weighty a matter for a simple Officer—"

"If you don't tell her, I'll do it myself," another manager interrupted.

"Very well." Gavin's bronze head returned to Carrie. He blinked. "Carrie, my dear, in return for the release of the captured marsoliie, the placktoids are asking for you."

CHAPTER TWENTY-TWO – A FRIEND IN NEED

Carrie missed Dave that night more than she had ever missed him before. Despite their reconciliation, he had obviously decided to stay in Belinda's cabin for the rest of their time aboard. The half-dandrobian probably picked up after herself, Carrie mused.

She sighed and turned over. From her new position, she could see through the cabin window to the ocean outside. They were at a latitude where the sun didn't set, and the daylight that shone through the water had dimmed but not entirely disappeared. She was hoping to see the small creatures that flashed in detailed patterns, or some other kind of interesting ocean life, but all was still except for ribbons of dark material that occasionally floated past, and vague shadowy shapes too far distant to make out clearly. If only she'd had the opportunity to explore the planet properly and find out all about the seventeen sentient species that lived there...now it looked as though that would never happen.

They were far from the placktoid base, but the mechanical aliens felt dreadfully near. She'd seen the maw of the shredder placktoid close up before and it was vivid in her mind. She could also clearly hear the cacophonous din of offkey classical music the placktoids created when speaking with other species.

Gavin had outlined the placktoid proposal gently and with many assurances that the Council Managers only wanted to keep her informed in case the placktoids decided to attack, because then she would be in particular danger, though of course the Unity would do everything to protect her. It was simple: the placktoids had identified her as the person who had exposed them. Due to her, a much-respected commander was imprisoned beneath oootoon. Their communication stated only that if the Council handed her over, they would release the marsoliie. What they would do with her, or to her, they didn't explain, though it was safe to conclude it wouldn't be anything she would enjoy.

Why the placktoids didn't simply open a gateway on the ship and storm it, no one understood for sure, but probably they weren't that confident in their firepower just yet, and perhaps they had intelligence about the new weapons that pierced their armour. If Carrie arrived at the placktoid base, unarmed, within twenty-hours, the mechanical aliens would return to wherever it was they were hiding.

There was no question of giving herself up, no question, Gavin had assured her. Carrie didn't think the rest of the managers were in full agreement. It was only one life against many, and the Unity battleships were still days out.

Gavin had also explained there was no easy escape for her. Wherever they sent her, the placktoids would probably find her, just as they had found out she was on Gaginion. If she went home to Earth, she would be exposing her home planet to a placktoid invasion.

As yet, the Unity had no plan for rescuing the marsoliie. Any attack on the base put their lives at risk. Carrie turned onto her back and stared at the ceiling. No matter what Gavin said, the solution seemed obvious. They were just waiting for her to say it. She closed her eyes and wished she hadn't driven Dave away with her bad behaviour and messy habits.

***

Audrey opened her door after only one ring of her doorbell.

"I hope I didn't wake you," said Carrie. She needed someone to talk to, and Audrey was the closest friend she had aboard after Dave and Gavin, both of whom she had annoyed enough already.

"Oh no, we don't sleep. Come in."

"You don't sleep?" She went into the green blob's cabin. "What do you do during rest periods?"

"Just bounce around, mostly."

Judging by the number of round, green imprints on Audrey's walls, she did a lot of bouncing.

"Is something bothering you?" Audrey asked.

"Yes, quite a bit actually. Do you mind if I hang out here for a while?"

"Be my guest," said Audrey as she bounced off the ceiling.

Carrie had been sworn to secrecy by the Managers. She supposed it was because they didn't know how the other trainees might react. Maybe they would gang up on her and tell her to give herself up to save the marsoliie. She hadn't really recovered her reputation after Belinda's damning account at the plenary session. But Carrie had never been good at keeping secrets, and she had got to know Audrey quite well over the week. She thought she could trust her, especially when it came to the question of possibly sacrificing herself to vicious mechanical aliens.

As her story unfolded, Audrey stopped bouncing. She rolled to a rest next to Carrie, where she listened, vibrating gently.

"So, that's it," Carrie concluded. "If I don't give myself over to them, hundreds of marsoliie will die."

"You aren't going to do it, are you?"

Carrie shrugged. "I don't see what else I can do."

"No. You can't. You mustn't. It would be stupid. It would only encourage the placktoids. We can't let them win at anything." Audrey wobbled in agitation.

"That's what the Managers said. *We must never give in to terrorists.* But isn't negotiation what our job's about? Bargaining? Give and take?"

"Not giving and taking lives," exclaimed Audrey.

Carrie shook her head. "I don't know. Maybe you're right. You're a much better Officer than me." She put her face in her hands. "What am I going to do?"

"I can't believe they even told you. That's a terrible responsibility to put on someone."

"They said it was for my protection. So I would know, if we were attacked, that they were coming for me."

Audrey rolled around the room. "I don't understand. If they want you, why not just come and get you? Why complicate things?"

"The Managers said they think it's because they aren't confident yet. They don't want to risk it. This way, if I give myself up, they won't suffer any casualties. But they know the Unity battleships are on their way, so I have to hand myself over by the deadline or they kill the marsoliie."

Audrey began rolling again. "Maybe there's a middle way. So we can save the marsoliie without losing you."

"I've been thinking about that too. But I've wracked my brains for hours without coming up with anything. If we or the Unity approach the placktoid station with weapons, they'll be able to detect them and they'll hurt the marsoliie. If I go in there with no weapons, that's it for me. But at least the marsoliie go free."

"I wouldn't bet on it. This is the placktoids we're talking about, remember? Once they have you, there's nothing to stop them destroying the marsoliie and disappearing through a transgalactic gateway, back to wherever it is they came from."

"You're right. But what else can we do? This is no good," said Carrie, standing up. "There isn't any answer. I should get back to my cabin. Maybe I'll get some sleep. Thanks for listening." What she actually intended was different from what she told Audrey. She intended to go straight to the nearest airlock and swim out into the ocean, where the placktoids could pick her up. That way, it would be clear no one had forced her to take the decision, and no one could stop her. At least the marsoliie might have a chance that way.

"Sit down. Don't give up yet. We have some of the best, most diverse trainee Officers right here aboard this ship. Between us, we must be able to find a way."

Carrie hesitated. She sat down. A few more hours one way or another, what difference would it make?

***

When Carrie burst into the staff office the following morning, she found Dave arguing loudly with them. At the sight of her, he raised a finger to stop her speaking. His eyes were like steel. "You're not doing it."

How had he found out? Maybe Gavin had told him. "Yes, I am."

"No way. I'll tie you to the ship if I have to. I'll, I'll—"

"No, you don't understand. I've got a plan. Or, actually, we've got a plan. Audrey and I thought it up last night."

"Ahem," said Gavin, "would this happen to be anything like the plan you had on the squashpump planet? Because I would not say that plan was particularly well thought out."

"No, not like the plan on the squashpump planet. We've thought it through carefully, together. Step by step. It might actually work." Seeing Dave's expression, she amended her words. "It will work, I'm sure of it."

"No," said Dave. "I know what you're like. You're just going to go off on one of your hare-brained escapades. But this is serious, Carrie. Your life is at risk. I'm not going to let you do it."

"You're not going to...?" She put her hands on her hips. Her voice rose. "Who do you think you are, telling me what I can and can't..." She caught herself, closed her eyes for a moment, and continued, "I know you're worried about me, Dave. And you have every right to be. I've been stupid, and reckless, and an idiot. But I've learned my lesson. This plan will work. I know it will. We can free the marsoliie, I won't be harmed, and we can get the placktoids back for what they've done."

CHAPTER TWENTY-THREE – SINK OR SWIM

Somewhere, out in the dark ocean, somewhere nearby, the Unity ship waited. Or, at least, Carrie hoped it did. She couldn't see it, but then she wouldn't expect to. A ship full of brave soldiers, who would swoop in and rescue her before the placktoids...she gulped.

The mechanical aliens had specified a distance of one click and no closer for the Council and Unity vessels, and that Carrie had to travel without the aid of a water scooter or any other vehicle in which she could hide a weapon. They had also said she could bring nothing with her: no toolbox, no devices, only a translator so that she could hear their court judgement, presumably before they...she swallowed again.

One click was quite a distance, and she had a long swim ahead of her, and only one respirator tablet to last her the whole trip. The placktoids' demands had been explicit: no additional items to be carried on her person, not even the tablets she needed to stay alive. The indicator needle was on the far left, so the tablet was completely fresh. One less thing to worry about, for the time being at least.

Far off, an upside-down, scarlet teardrop

swayed like a hot air balloon at a fair. The large net of trapped marsoliie. Below it, very unlike a fair, sat the placktoid base. Carrie recognised the cubic, featureless buildings she had first seen on Oootoon. Lacking all decoration or ornament, they indicated to her, hopefully, the placktoids' lack of imagination.

Gavin had told Carrie once, before they understood how evil the placktoids were, that they deserved the same consideration and respect as every other civilisation in the galaxy. He'd said they had culture and an obscure history, during which their original creators had been lost to knowledge. Just because they were mechanical, that did not mean they weren't sentient nor entitled to the same rights as other intelligent species.

Gazing at the patch of floodlit ground where the placktoids awaited her, Carrie wondered what Gavin thought of them now.

It was difficult for her to swim encased as she was in Audrey's huge wetsuit. She imagined she must look like a blimp, with only the bottom halves of her arms and legs poking out. Her legs began aching with the effort of kicking when she had such little room to move. As she swam steadily on, she hoped the placktoids wouldn't think it strange that she had grown noticeably larger. But as they seemed to have watched plenty of Earth TV she had her fingers crossed that they were familiar with the fact that humans sometimes became excessively overweight.

She glanced over her shoulder. In the Council

ship portholes were faces. Dave, Gavin, Audrey, the blinking light, even Belinda had come to see her off. Though had the half-dandrobian only turned up to make sure she left? Whatever. She was grateful for the emotional support. Most of all, she was happy she had parted from Dave on good terms. If she were not to return, he would have good memories of her.

She shivered and shook her head. She needed to keep a positive outlook. The plan was a good one, with a better than average chance of succeeding. She looked over her shoulder again. The Council ship looked much smaller now. She must have covered about half the distance. She just needed to stay calm, think carefully and follow the plan through step by step. No rash, reckless behaviour.

As she drew nearer to the placktoid base, Carrie took a look around into the ocean depths. Anything to avoid seeing the placktoids until the last minute when she would have to face them. The water was dim. The dark ribbon shapes she had seen the previous night swam past in the distance to her right, and she thought she could detect, farther on, a patch of the sentient mat that floated on the ocean surface, which she had encountered on her first foray into the water. Above, the green light from the alien sun looked friendly and inviting, though she knew the atmosphere meant death. There were no marsoliie to be seen. Carrie didn't blame them for not approaching the area where their friends and relations were being held captive. She hoped the Groups in the net were leaving the Singles alone.

Her breath was labouring. Swimming in the massive wetsuit was much harder than she had imagined. Her respirator indicator needle was approaching the centre. She tried to breathe more shallowly, but she needed all the oxygen she could get to keep going.

There was movement ahead. Glinting in the diffuse light, large placktoid paperclips were patrolling the perimeter of the base. Their hovering motion made Carrie shiver as she recalled how she had first travelled inside one as it took her up to the placktoid ship. She had been so ignorant, so naive at the time, it was a wonder she hadn't got herself and Dave killed. But that was then. This was now. This was a different Carrie, who meant business.

A paperclip was growing larger. It was zooming out to meet her. She stopped swimming. Finally, she was able to rest her aching legs as she waited for it. Her breathing slowed. Thank goodness. She was going to need all the oxygen her respirator tablet contained.

The placktoid didn't speak, at least not to her. It might have been transmitting to its superiors at the base. Instead, it floated in front of her and began to vibrate, disturbing the water surrounding it. The familiar attractive force drew Carrie into its centre where she floated, contained within an invisible forcefield, while the paperclip completed her journey to the placktoid commander. Once there, she would be given over to it to do with as it pleased, or so it thought.

During the short final leg, she used the time to collect her thoughts and go over each step carefully in her mind. The first step and the most important was to take place outside the base. This was where it would be a disaster if things didn't go according to plan. She had to be released from the forcefield at the entrance to the base. There was no logical reason that prevented the paperclip from carrying her inside and directly through to the commander, but previously, on Oootoon, the paperclips had always dropped her, Dave and Belinda at the entrance to the ship, never carrying them inside.

Carrie hoped that Gavin was right, that the placktoids had culture, habits and ways of behaving that were not purely logical.

They were nearly at the base. The doors opened as the paperclip slowed down. Carrie's heart rose into her mouth. Would it carry her right inside? If the forcefield wasn't deactivated while she was outside the base...She began to sweat. Through the open doors she could see only darkness. The square, empty entrance loomed larger.

At the very last second, just inside the threshold, she was released. She fell to the base floor, pulled down by the weight of the wetsuit and its contents, but the contents cushioned her fall well. That was the least of her concerns. Her back tickled as the trainee squashpump, clad in a scrap of Unity uniform, slid up her back and out the neck of her suit. She had left her hair untied to give it as much cover as she could, but she dared not reach round to help it nor give any other indication of its presence to the placktoids awaiting her. Would the squashpump make it out in time? She couldn't feel it anymore. It must have been glided down the outside of her wetsuit. Behind her, the doors slid closed. Her heart thumping, she prayed the slug-like alien hadn't been caught between them.

"Stay where you are," said a large placktoid that resembled a staple remover. She had always hated their metal teeth. "Open your facial orifice."

Carrie assumed it meant her mouth. She opened wide. A light beamed into her mouth from a biro-like placktoid that rested on its nib nearby.

"DNA match confirmed. This is the human named Carrie Hatchett," said the biro.

DNA? How did the placktoids know her DNA? She had spent some time aboard their ship, imprisoned in a cell with Dave, but the ship had crashed into the oootoon ocean. Unless the placktoids who escaped had taken a sample of her genetic code with them? They were even more vengeful and devious than she'd thought. But on the other hand it was a good sign. If they were checking her DNA to identify her, perhaps they weren't relying on identifying her through appearance, which was vastly different from normal.

Glancing down at her respirator indicator, her chest tightened. The needle had left the centre and was working its way to the right. Had the squashpump made it outside? Was it on its way to complete its task? Would it manage to do it in time before her oxygen ran out?

"Locomote through here," said the staple remover. It moved to a metallic archway.

"You mean swim?" asked Carrie. She moved towards the arch. "What is this thing?"

"Do as directed."

"It's a weapon scanner, right?"

"Do as directed or you will be immediately destroyed."

"I'm moving, I'm moving," said Carrie, increasing her speed, wobbling as she went. She certainly had no reason to delay. She had no time to lose. But if this was a weapon scanner, and she had every reason to believe it was, now was the crunch time.

She closed her eyes and passed beneath the arch, her heartbeat resounding in her ears. When she came out the other side she stopped, hardly daring to breathe. Opening her eyes, she saw the placktoids hadn't moved. No alarm seemed to have gone off. The plan had worked, so far.

CHAPTER TWENTY-FOUR – CRUNCH TIME

The commander at the placktoid base was every bit as terrifying as the one Carrie had helped send to indefinite confinement on Oootoon. Its steel maw faced her, a bank of knife-like teeth. Behind the maw lay the long, rectangular box section of the 'shredder', though she doubted it held the remains of out-of-date or confidential office documents. Along the sides were the caterpillar treads she vividly remembered churning when she was chased aboard the placktoid ship. Particularly sharp in her mind was dreadful wrenching, grinding sound of the commander's engine at full throttle.

It was the size of the thing that really made her heart quail. Had she underestimated the magnitude of the first one she had seen? She could hardly believe it. She'd heard the mind exaggerated when it came to objects of deepest fear, not underestimated them. If this new commander really was substantially larger, she might be in trouble. There might not be enough —

"Carrie Hatchett," the commander's deep bass voice boomed. "You have been tried by the Court of the New Social Order and found guilty of treason and false imprisonment. Your sentence is—"

"Wait, what? What's the New Social Order? I've never heard of it. The Unity and Transgalactic Council don't recognise this body." Clearly, the placktoid commander wasn't going to hang around before administering her punishment. What happened to the long speeches given by the baddies that allowed the hero time to escape? Hadn't it watched Earth TV? She had to stall it, to delay the discharge of her sentence, for obvious reasons, but also to give the squashpump time to do its work.

"The New Social Order is the legitimate galactic government, soon to become historical fact. Your collusion with the oootoon has been thoroughly witnessed, recorded and documented. There is no doubt you are responsible for the illegal apprehension and confinement of placktoid commander 783. Your sentence is—"

"No, that's wrong. There is no galactic government. The Unity and Council work in partnership to supervise and administrate galactic affairs. Anyway, what do you mean, *soon to become* historical fact? It's either historical fact or it isn't." She was stalling, of course, but her curiosity was also piqued and the commander's words pierced the numbing terror that threatened to overwhelm her. "Isn't it?" Inside her helmet, sweat trickled down her face, not only due to the padding in her wetsuit. *Stay calm, Carrie. One step at a time.*

"The Unity and Transgalactic Council have also contravened the tenets of the New Social Order, and they shall be dealt with in due course."

"Ha, you plan to take on the Unity? You'll never do it. They have the most advanced technology there is; the very best that every civilisation has to offer. You think the placktoids alone can beat the might of the entire galaxy?" Carrie wondered if she'd heard that line in a movie once. She shook her head. Her terror was making her mind wander. She needed to concentrate, now most of all. What was the squashpump up to? Why was it taking so long?

"Only the placktoids have the right and the might to lead the galaxy to its supreme manifestation and out into the universe. But that magnificent future is shortly to become no concern of yours, Carrie Hatchett. You are sentenced to..."

Carrie grimaced and took a step back. If she acted now, she might have a tiny chance at saving herself, but for the plan to work she had to wait. Glancing to right and left, she saw there were no other placktoids in the room. Presumably the commander was planning on carrying out her sentence itself. But why wasn't it saying anything?

"No. That cannot be," said the commander. "How? Recapture them at once." Carrie's heart leapt. The commander was clearly responding to an electronic communication from another placktoid, but in its confusion it was also speaking to her. Its words were all she needed. The squashpump had made it. It had climbed the placktoid base and reached the net holding the marsoliie. Applying a magnetic field neutraliser, it had opened the lock, releasing the net and setting the marsoliie free.

Finally, it was her turn to act. She ran toward the mechanical alien and tore down the zip on Audrey's massive wetsuit. The oootoon confined within spilled out over the floor and beneath the commander's steel teeth in a yellow tide. The placktoid commander took a second too long to recognise it and realise what was happening. Its caterpillar treads started up and it sped backwards, away from it nemesis. But it was too late. A tendril of oootoon had reached it, and the rest soon flowed in; into its treads, its engine and other inner workings, where it began to solidify. The commander started forward, apparently trying to attack Carrie with its last free movement. But the oootoon worked too fast. The placktoid jerked to a halt. It lurched back, and forward again before it froze, immobilised by the oootoon.

"Yay, we did it. We've got it now. Hold tight, hold tight, don't let go. Don't let go of what? Oh dear, someone isn't paying attention. Just stay still, we'll explain later. All right."

Carrie hoped the oootoon could also prevent the commander from communicating with the rest of the placktoids, but she hoped in vain. Its mechanical subordinates poured into the room. Darting around the side of the immobile shredder for protection, Carrie pulled two of the new weapons from her swimsuit. Thank goodness the placktoids' scanner had been unable to penetrate the oootoon and find them. She leaned out, a weapon in each hand, and concentrated with all her might to fire them. She scored two hits. There were so many placktoids it was difficult to miss. True to their promise the high-energy beams sliced through the mechanical aliens, searing their innards. As their comrades fell in pieces the remaining placktoids hesitated, seemingly surprised and dismayed by the carnage Carrie had caused.

Hope lifted her spirits. The placktoids were not firing at her. Presumably they didn't want to risk hurting their beloved commander. If she could just hold them off long enough. Now the marsoliie were free, the placktoids had no hostage protection. The Unity ship must be on its way. Sure enough, as the realisation formed in Carrie's mind, an explosion hit the base and rocked it. The Unity had arrived. Placktoids were sent toppling to the floor.

Taking advantage of their plight, Carrie leaned out and fired again, wielding yet more damage to the upended placktoids. But then their confused behaviour changed, and they rose as one. Carrie guessed that, unheard by her, the commander was communicating with his troops, rallying them to attack. They turned together and advanced towards her position.

Another explosion rocked the base, tumbling her through the water and knocking both weapons from her hands. Her ears rang with the boom that resounded. She scrambled for the weapons and managed to grab one as she sighted a placktoid zooming towards her. She cut it down with a burst of fire, but her hope plummeted. They were on both sides of the shredder now, surrounding her.

"Hurry, please hurry," she murmured. A placktoid appeared in front of her. She fired and whirled around just in time to destroy another that approached her from behind. Where were the Unity troops? Surely they must have got into the base by now? Unless they thought she would never make it. Unless they had given up on her and were just going to destroy the base.

Carrie swallowed her fear and dived for the second weapon. She glided through the water, grabbed it, turned onto her back and fired with both hands simultaneously, hitting two placktoids square in the middle. One fell apart and stopped moving, but the other continued to advance, even though its top half lay twitching on the floor behind it. Carrie fired again, searing a hole through it, but still the placktoid approached, her hit only slowing it down.

Sensing movement behind, she whirled round to mow down three mechanical aliens that were nearly upon her. A metal arm grabbed her. The wounded placktoid had reached her. She spun and kicked out at it, propelling it against the commander's side. It rebounded and flew at her head. She ducked. The placktoid hit the wall behind her, denting the metal. A watery clunk echoed through Carrie's helmet. Still the placktoid moved. As it advanced again, Carrie leapt to meet it. She reached inside it as deep as her arm would go, grabbed a handful of wires, and yanked. As the wires came free, finally, the placktoid stopped.

But it wasn't enough. More of the mechanical aliens were coming up, and behind them, still more. It was no good. She would never get them all. She slumped against the wall, a weapon in either hand. Her vision was blurry, and she felt dizzy and faint.

Was this it, then? Was this how she was going to die? Ah well, at least the marsoliie were safe. It was a shame she didn't get to tell Gavin what the placktoid commander had said. But never mind, they would probably figure it out soon enough.

The placktoids were nearly upon her. Her eyes slowly closed. The last thing she saw was her respirator indicator needle. It was on the far right. She was out of air.

CHAPTER TWENTY-FIVE – SURPRISE AWAKENING

Hearing was the first of Carrie's senses to return. Her ears were ringing. She also heard bubbles and swishes. She was still underwater. She forced her eyes open. Above was a ceiling—the ceiling of the placktoid base. She hadn't moved from where she had fallen. Yet she was still alive. The placktoids she had last seen moving in hadn't killed her. She drew in a deep breath. Sweet air filled her lungs, sending energy coursing through her. Oxygen. Someone had replaced her respirator tablet. Probably the same someone whose arms she felt about her, supporting her shoulders and head.

Rapid communications sounded through her helmet radio. Orders and spurts of information. She was too dazed. She couldn't understand what they were talking about.

She blinked and squinted, forcing her eyes to focus. Who was holding her? The person was out of her immediate view. Was it Dave? Had he come to find her in the wreckage of the placktoid base? She twisted her head to see the person's face, but all she saw was the opaque visor of a Unity soldier. Her heart sank. She was relieved to be alive, but she felt a burning need for a familiar face.

"Hatchett's coming round," called a voice.

It was a woman's voice. It seemed to come from the soldier holding her. Carrie recognised the voice. After a few moments, she made the connection. "B—Belinda?"

The helmeted figure nodded.

"You..." Carrie struggled out of the half-dandrobian's grasp, and in her weakened state began to float away. She steadied herself against the wall. "You saved me?"

Belinda shrugged. "I suppose you could say that. We were all searching the base for you, trying to locate you before the decision was made to blow the place sky high. We only had a couple of minutes left before we had to give up the search because we knew your respirator tablet would be exhausted. I saw the placktoid wreckage spilling from the door and figured only you could have created it. As soon as I saw the commander I knew I had the right place. Called in my buddies and saw you here behind him. We put an end to the placktoids you hadn't managed to polish off. Just in time, it seems."

Carrie surveyed the wreckage that lay before her, the remains of the placktoid commander. The Unity soldiers had taken no chances in destroying the mechanical alien. It was unrecognisable. If she hadn't seen it before the soldiers started work, she wouldn't have been able to guess what it used to be. The Unity did not mess around. Floating through the door on their way out were long ribbon strands of oootoon. She would speak to it later to thank it for doing a brilliant job.

She tried to stand, but dizziness overcame her.

"Rest a while, Hatchett," said Belinda. "You were out cold when I found you. I don't know how long you went without oxygen. Your tablet was nothing but powder when I replaced it."

A chill settled on Carrie. She had come so close to death. If Belinda hadn't found her... "But, what are you doing here? How come you aren't back on the Council ship? Have you rejoined the Unity?"

Belinda shook her helmeted head. "I asked to take part in the attack and they let me, for old times' sake."

"The attack." Carrie recalled the explosions she'd felt inside the base. "What happened?"

"The second the marsoliie were out of danger, the gunship started firing. The return fire was potent, and the ship sustained significant damage. If it weren't for the fact that we fired first, we might not have beaten them, but we managed to take out their main defenses.

"Our fighter ships moved in, too, and got most of the placktoids that streamed out of the base. There weren't many. Once they were down, us foot soldiers advanced into the base to find you, like I said. But apart from the commander and the other placktoids in here, the base was almost entirely deserted."

"But I saw lots when I came in," said Carrie.

"Are you sure they checked the whole base?"

Belinda nodded. "It looks like most of them retreated through a gateway as soon as they knew the fight was lost and their commander was trapped by oootoon."

"They left through a transgalactic gateway again." Carrie frowned. The placktoids had returned to their hideout, wherever that was. Thinking back to her short conversation with the commander, she had a suspicion his odd comments might hold the clue as to where that hideout was. If she was right, she needed to speak to Gavin and the other Managers. "I'm feeling better, Belinda. I think I can swim back now. I'm getting pretty chilly, too." Audrey's deflated wetsuit sagged around her, its zip open where she had released the oootoon. She struggled out of it. Wearing only her swimsuit, she shivered in the cool water. "I need to get back to the Council ship."

"Okay, I'll come with you." Carrie and the half-dandrobian set off through the placktoid base. As they approached the exit, Belinda said, "I heard you were terrible during target practice. No one held out much hope for you once the commander realised the game was up. But I saw you put paid to a fair few placktoids before your respirator tablet gave out. Well done."

"Thanks," said Carrie. She thought she could get used to this new, friendly Belinda. "You know, I found my aim improved considerably when I thought I was about to die."

"Hmm...that's often the case, or if it isn't, you

don't get to hear about it."

***

Outside the base, Carrie saw with grim satisfaction, was the wreckage of the staple remover. The Unity attack had reduced it to scrap metal. Nearby were pieces of paperclip and other bits of placktoid she didn't recognise.

"Good t' see ye made it."

Carrie spun round. It took her a moment to spot the squashpump halfway up the entrance wall. "I'm glad to see you made it, too." Her fears had been greatest for this small officer trainee. At any moment it might have been spotted scaling the wall or searching for and releasing the mechansim that held the marsoliie captive. The placktoids would have picked it off easily. And once the attack started, it could have been hit at any time. She'd had the protection of the building at least. "You were so brave."

"Och, there wasna much chance of yon placktoids seeing me. Us squashpumps often get overlooked because of our size, y' know. I was glad o' the chance t' help out."

"We couldn't have done it without you." The slug-like aliens were tough little fellows.

Carrie shivered. She was seriously cold now. "See you back at the ship." The Council starship had drawn near, and she could see the Unity ship too. The placktoid weapons had destroyed its camouflage device and now it was easy to see. For a simple Unity gunship, it was impressive. Twice the size of the Council ship, it was sleek and glistening where it wasn't blackened by placktoid fire. The sight of it gave her heart for the galactic war that threatened. The placktoids may have gateway technology, but the Unity forces would still take some beating.

With the Council ship much nearer, Carrie didn't face the long swim she had made in getting to the placktoid base, and she was no longer hampered by Audrey's wetsuit filled with oootoon. But despite these facts, she found herself swimming slowly. Belinda kept pace beside her, not speaking, probably thinking she was exhausted from the trials of the day. The truth was, as she swam, she was taking another long look at the ocean surrounding her.

She would no doubt be sent home soon along with the other trainees. Her outlook had changed considerably in the last few hours. Now she knew it might not be the last time she would get to see the underwater world of the marsoliie and other sentient creatures of Gaginion. No Groups or Singles remained, but in the distance she saw an edge of the massive floating mat and other sea creatures she hadn't seen before. She took in the underwater view, fixing it in her memory until perhaps, one day, when they had defeated the placktoids, she could return.

CHAPTER TWENTY-SIX – RECONCILIATION

When Carrie got back to the Council ship, the first person she looked for as she stepped out of the airlock was Dave, but he was nowhere to be seen. Audrey was there, and she enveloped Carrie in a large, blobby hug. The oootoon had also made its way back after draining out of the placktoid commander and had returned to its box, where it appeared to be none the worse for wear. The other trainees formed a welcoming party, and as Carrie was hugged, slapped, jiggled, bumped and subjected to the various species' other forms of congratulations, she felt both undeserving in comparison with the bravery of the oootoon and the squashpump, and slightly hurt. Where was Dave? Why hadn't her best friend appeared? She'd thought they had reconciled, but maybe he was still angry with her.

As soon as she could be extracted from the trainees, Carrie was whisked away to a debriefing session with Gavin, Errruorerrrrrhch and the other managers. She was still in her swimsuit, but Errruorerrrrrhch gave her a blanket to wrap herself in. The managers wanted to know what had happened, detail by detail, what she had seen inside the placktoid base, and exactly what the placktoids had said to her. Knowing that any clue as to where the placktoids were hiding out was vital, Carrie concentrated hard to remember and tell them everything she could, no matter how small or insignificant it might have seemed at the time. But she thought she already knew the placktoids' whereabouts, and after hearing what the commander had said to her, the managers were inclined to agree with her conclusion. They made her promise to keep the news confidential, however, at least for the time being, until the Transgalactic Council received the information from Carrie's debriefing and decided on their next move.

Exhaustion overwhelmed her as she left the Central Office. The corridors of the starship were silent. It seemed the trainees were at a meal or other activity. After all the hubbub at her return and the long questioning by the Council Managers, Carrie was grateful for the peace and quiet. In all the excitement she had lost track of time, and the view from the portholes gave little indication as to whether it was lunchtime or late evening. She yawned and rubbed her eyes and decided to go back to her room. Maybe Dave would be there. If he wasn't she could get a little sleep at least.

Her cabin was exactly as she had left it that morning. She picked up her pyjamas from off the floor and changed out of her swimsuit. She took a quick shower, returning the wet towel to the shower room before getting into bed and falling quickly into a deep sleep.

The next thing she knew someone was waking her. Opening her eyes a slit, she saw Dave's face peering at her. Turning away from him, she murmured, "I'll get up in a minute. You go to breakfast without me."

"Carrie, it's evening."

"What?" She forced her eyes open. Remembering the day's events, she turned back to her friend. "What are you doing here?" She sat up. "And where have you been? I thought you'd be here when I got back. Where did you go?"

He grinned. "Sorry, I meant to be back in time to see you, but I had other things to do. Get up and I'll show you what I mean."

"All right. Give me a minute." Carrie gave a stretch, easing her tired muscles from her long swim. She pushed back her blankets, swung her legs over the edge of the bunk and jumped down. She looked curiously at her friend's secret, triumphant expression. "I don't suppose you're going to tell me what this is about."

"Just get dressed. I'll wait for you outside."

As soon as she was ready, Dave took her hand and led her through the ship.

"Hey," Carrie said, "did you know Belinda saved my life?"

"Yeah, I heard. She's pretty cool when you get to know her."

They entered an area unfamiliar to Carrie. As they stepped through an open door she gasped. "I never knew this place existed. Why didn't they tell us about it?" The room was like a small lecture theatre, with seats and other furniture designed to accommodate a range of species, though it wasn't large enough to seat the whole ship's complement. Instead of facing a podium, the audience looked out through a rounded, cone-shaped window into the sea beyond. Carrie was mildly annoyed. All the time that she had spent aboard the ship peering through small portholes, when she could have come to this observation deck and seen the starscape or ocean in all its splendour.

Her irritation melted away, however, in the face of the sight outside. The trainees and Council staff who had gathered there parted so that she and Dave could go to the front for a good view. The marsoliie had returned. Massive Groups floated just beyond the ship, pulsating and trembling in the ocean currents.

"Why are they here?" Carrie asked.

"Just watch," replied Dave. They had arrived just in time. Immediately after he spoke, the Groups began to break apart. Individual by individual, Singles detached from the whole, floating apart, until the ocean heaved with lone marsoliie like scarlet snowflakes that danced but never fell.

"Wow," said Carrie. She itched to be out among the beautiful, fluttering creatures. She turned to her friend. "So the marsoliie all decided to be Singles?"

"Not quite. It isn't over yet. Just wait a while. I think you'll see something very special."

Returning to the view, Carrie saw two Singles rejoin. A third came to join them and attached itself. Then a fourth and a fifth. The new Group began to lazily spin, and another Single approached to become one with the ball. Other Singles were joining ranks, forming larger and larger Groups. These swam among the crowd, as if inviting more Singles into their midst.

Carrie rested her elbows on the window, her eyes following the beautiful and mysterious movement. After some time, the , the ocean was filled with a mixture of Groups and Singles. Then the marsoliie began to disperse.

"Oh, I think I get it," said Carrie.

"Do you?" asked Dave.

Carrie frowned. "Actually, I don't get it at all. Why did the Groups split apart just to join up again? And how come they aren't chasing the Singles any more?"

"Well done, Dave," said Gavin as he approached. "It must feel gratifying to witness the results of your efforts."

Carrie's friend smiled broadly. "Yes, it is."

"Dave would make an excellent Transgalactic Intercultural Community Crisis Liaison Officer, Carrie," said Gavin. "I am pleased that he accompanied you on previous assignments, even as an unauthorised companion. He clearly possesses an excellent range of skills. Thank you for introducing him to the Council. In the forthcoming fight with the placktoids, we will need all the expertise we can acquire."

"Is one of you going to tell me what's going on?" asked Carrie.

"Oh, are you unaware what your companion accomplished? When the marsoliie were released from the placktoids' net, only Groups remained. It was apparent that during their time of imprisonment all of the Singles had been assimilated, undoubtedly against their will. Their confinement allowed them no opportunity to escape.

"Seeing this, Dave volunteered himself to approach and reason with these Groups before they dispersed into the ocean. As a result of his excellent efforts at intervention and negotiation, the Groups took it upon themselves to separate. Only those Singles who actively approached others would reform into a Group, while others who did not were free to resume their individual lifestyles."

"That's where you went," exclaimed Carrie. Dave smiled.

"It is a rare officer who can, with such speed, facilitate a positive, mutually agreed outcome," said Gavin. "Such self-originating agreements are the most stable and long-lasting, and they are the pinnacle of achievement in the business of mediating in intercultural community crises."

Carrie patted her friend on the back, swallowing a certain amount of jealousy. Gavin was right, it was a great achievement, and Dave would make a great officer. She just wished she was equally good at the job and didn't constantly blunder through her assignments, succeeding only through luck.

A knot formed in her stomach. The training course was over and they would soon hear who had passed and who had failed. Despite the positive outcome with the placktoids, Carrie still held grave doubts she would be returned to duty. From the deep brain scan results, through her various gaffes during training, to her confession to Gavin that she had stolen a weapon, she assumed she would be gently advised—or ordered—to resign, if she wasn't outright sacked.

She didn't want to become a Unity soldier as Belinda had. Though she loved travelling across the galaxy and meeting alien species, her experience with the placktoids had been terrifying. She sparred in Bagua Zhang for fun and exercise, not because she liked fighting. It looked like her career was over.

CHAPTER TWENTY-SEVEN – THE PLACKTOIDS' PLAN

Their bags were packed and Carrie and Dave were back in their ordinary, Earth clothes. They were waiting in their cabin for Errruorerrrrhch to come and talk to them about the training week before they returned home. Farewells in the canteen after breakfast had been emotional. The trainees were unsure of when they might see each other again. Liaison Officers generally worked remotely and rarely went to the Transgalactic Council offices or met staff other than their direct managers. And Carrie was sure that this would be her last time aboard a starship; her last encounter with a Council Manager; her last venture into space. She had burst into tears as she had tried to get her arms around Audrey to give her a proper hug. The green blob had literally saved her life. She could never have come up with the plan to fool the placktoids on her own.

Now she was sniffing and wiping her eyes as she checked the cabin for anything she might have missed. As she was crouching to look under the bunk she gave a particularly loud sniff.

Dave sighed. "It'll be good to see Toodles and

Rogue again, won't it?" he said. Carrie didn't answer. After a pause he continued, "As soon as we get back, the first thing I'm going to do is brew a cuppa, then I'm going to eat something, anything, that tastes like normal food." When Carrie still didn't answer, he added, "You haven't got any biscuits, have you?" and chuckled.

Carrie sat back on her heels. "Thanks, Dave. I know what you're trying to do and I appreciate it, but it's okay. I am looking forward to seeing Toodles and Rogue and I'll be all right after a day or two. It was just that I really loved this job, and it's going to be hard to return to an ordinary life when I've travelled across the galaxy and met aliens, you know?"

"Huh? What makes you think you won't be working as a Liaison Officer?"

"I told you before, I'm going to fail the course. Gavin warned me."

"You're not still going on about that, are you? Are you mad? After what happened with the placktoids you think the Council's going to fail you?"

"That was a group effort. It wasn't just me. And it wasn't even my idea. Audrey thought up most of the plan. The only reason I was there was because it was me the placktoids wanted. It'd be nice to be able to take credit for the success, but I honestly can't, and even if I could it wasn't Liaison Officer work. It wasn't what we've been training in all week." She stood and went to the cabin window for a final look into space. The starship had left Gaginion overnight, and now outside all was black velvet dotted with brilliant, hard points of light. Off to starboard was a reddish-pink burst of gaseous nebula.

"Think about it, Dave. You can't blame them. I was terrible at nearly all the exercises. The only thing I could do well was swim. Swim! Even *I* wouldn't hire myself. I should never have strong-armed Gavin into taking me on." Carrie swallowed. It was time Dave knew the truth, the information she'd been withholding from him all week.

He tutted. "Look, for a start, Audrey said you contributed a lot to the plan, and most importantly you listened and you thought everything through before you did anything. You're being ridiculous—"

"There's something I haven't told you, as well." She turned to face her friend, her cheeks turning rosy. "During our first night on board, they scanned our brains to assess our mental compatibility with the Liaison Officer role. I got a really low score. Only thirty-four per cent."

"They scanned our brains without telling us? That isn't right."

"They did tell us, but you'd left the canteen by then and you were asleep by the time I got back here. Anyway, it's pretty clear from what's happened this week that the assessment was correct."

"I still think you're...hang on, I didn't see my result. Did you see it?"

Carrie hung her head. "Yes, I did see it but I

didn't tell you. I'm sorry. I was upset. You see, you scored ninety-seven."

"Ninety-seven." Dave's eyes widened and he smiled. "That's..." Seeing Carrie's expression he stumbled over his words. "I mean, that's..."

"It's okay. You did really well, and you'll make a great officer. Aren't you glad I made you come along?"

"Well, now that you mention—" The doorbell sounded. Errruorerrrrhch had arrived. But when Dave opened the door, Gavin was there.

"Hello, Carrie and Dave. My paternity leave has come to an end and I have resumed my duties. I am here to give you your feedback and send you home. I imagine you will both be looking forward to returning to Earth? Would you prefer me to speak to each of you in private?"

"Come in, Gavin," said Carrie, pleased to have this final encounter with her massive, bronze, insectoid Manager. "You can tell me the news in front of Dave, I don't mind."

"Good, good," replied Gavin as he eased himself into the room. "It would save time to speak to you together, providing Dave does not object?" Dave shook his head. "Very well. First of all, let me congratulate you on a successful training week. I hope you enjoyed the experience and derived benefit from it. Secondly—"

"You mean I passed?" exclaimed Carrie.

"But of course."

Carrie let out a whoop and punched the air.

She grabbed Dave and hugged him, then turned to Gavin and opened her arms to hug him too, but couldn't find a suitable place. She settled for kissing one of his antennae instead.

"It is most odd that you would imagine you had not passed the course."

"That's what I kept telling her," said Dave.

"But I only got thirty-four per cent on the brain scan."

"Per cent? You are mistaken. I understand your confusion now. The result of the scan is not expressed as a percentage. Perfect compatibility —the highest possible result—is zero. That is never achieved. Thirty-four is a very high score. I am guessing that perhaps you did not read through the information provided?"

"Oh, I, err..." Carrie's elation turned to embarrassment. She really would need to pay more attention in the future.

Dave rolled his eyes. "Did you have something else to tell us, Gavin?"

"Yes, indeed. Carrie, the Council and Unity have discussed the report you provided on your encounter with the placktoid commander and have come to the same conclusion that you yourself derived. This information is to remain completely confidential, however, so I must warn you that what I am about to say must not be passed on nor even hinted at to another sentient entity until you receive explicit permission to do so. I am able to inform Dave because I have a proposal for you both to consider.

"But first, Dave, after your exemplary performance I am hoping you will accept the position of Transgalactic Intercultural Community Crisis Liaison Officer?"

"Well, I…" He ran his hand through his hair. "It's a bit risky, but this week's been a lot more fun than I thought it would be, catering provision aside. I suppose…"

Carrie held her hands to her chest, her fists clenched.

"I suppose so. Okay."

"Yes!" Carrie punched the air again, grabbed her friend's head, pulled it down and planted a kiss on his cheek.

"I am extremely pleased to hear that. You will be an invaluable member of the team, I am sure. Furthermore, due to the current crisis the Council is deploying its Officers in teams of two as an additional safety measure. You two would be expected to work as partners. Is that agreeable to you?"

"That would be brilliant," exclaimed Carrie.

"Hmm." Dave rubbed his chin. "Well, all right then." Carrie punched his arm and he chuckled.

"However," said Gavin as he lowered his head in a serious manner, "I must warn you that I have no forgotten the incident of the stolen weapon. Any further transgressions of a similar nature will result in your instant dismissal. I hope you both fully comprehend me?"

Carrie and Dave nodded solemnly. "But, wait a minute," said Carrie, "you told me someone was going to fail earlier. If it isn't me, who is it?"

"It was Bbbbbb. You remember the light? It was very aloof. It refused to have anything to do with any of the other trainees, and such an attitude is detrimental to effective service in the Liaison Officer role.

"Now, to the matter at hand. The intelligence gathered by Carrie has led us to believe we know where the placktoids are hiding. Indeed, it is the only reasonable explanation for their total disappearance, and, to be frank, there is some embarrassment regarding the fact that no one thought of the answer earlier."

"It isn't 'where', though, is it?" said Carrie.

"No indeed. Not where, but *when*. The reason we have not been able to locate the placktoids is because we have been looking for them in the present. In fact, they have gone back in time. Exactly what period of time has yet to be established. Their intention, according to the brief comment the placktoid commander made, seems to be to alter the events of history so that their species gains control of the galaxy from an earlier time period onward. Clearly they have not yet done so, or we would now be living under their dominion, if we were even to exist."

"Woah," said Dave. "I'm not sure I like the direction this is heading."

"You surmise correctly. I would like to propose that you and Carrie form the Liaison Officer contingent of the team we send back to find the placktoids and prevent them from executing their plan."

"We'd love to," exclaimed Carrie.

At the same time time, Dave said, "We'll think about it."

***

Her hands wrapped round a warm mug of tea, sitting in her kitchen and watching Rogue wolf down his food, Carrie contemplated the events of the previous week and the task that lay ahead. Dave had gone home, keen to relax and recover before another day's work at the call centre. She sipped her tea and wondered what they might find when they travelled back in time to the placktoids' hideout.

Putting down her mug, she patted Rogue as he came over to her after finishing his food. She smiled. Whatever lay ahead, she would try to think before she acted, and with Dave by her side everything would be okay.

Carrie's story continues in...

WRONG SIDE OF TIME

Sign up to my reader group for a free copy of *Carrie Hatchett's Christmas*, the standalone novelette in the Carrie Hatchett, Space Adventurer series, and for exclusive notice of new releases, advanced reader opportunities and other interesting stuff:

https://jjgreenauthor.com/free-books/

ALSO BY J.J. GREEN

STAR MAGE SAGA

SPACE COLONY ONE

SHADOWS OF THE VOID

LOST TO TOMORROW

THERE COMES A TIME
A SCIENCE FICTION
COLLECTION

DAWN FALCON
A FANTASY COLLECTION